Love Stories Your Momma Never Read

Love Stories Your Momma Never Read

by

Dennis J. Reader

www.sempervirensbooks.com

Published 2023 by Sempervirens Books

Cover artwork by Nicole Reader

Cover graphics by GDM

ISBN (paperback) 979-8-9855825-4-3

ISBN (ebook) 979-8-9855825-5-0

FOR FURTHER INFORMATION OR OTHER BOOKS BY THE AUTHOR GO TO:
www.sempervirensbooks.com

---Contents---

The Middle of the End

I reside now, a childless widower, in the shiny new cottage condo complex of Casa del Sol. Interesting, here out west in the USA, that when a condo gets titled a *casa,* the Spanish adds 15% to the cost of a lease. But no complaints—this housing project shows quality everywhere, a top-drawer retirement in the sun, seniors-only please, age sixty minimum.

Right off I observed that most of my fellow occupants easily qualify over the sixty mark with the majority being single women. In that regard the actuarial tables play in my favor, since I lost my own wife thirteen years ago, and she taught me well the values of living with the right woman.

Mrs. Simmons of Unit 1002 was the first at my door, coming before I finished unpacking. In her gloved hands she held a piping hot casserole of five different cheeses, the recipe a special blend, she explained in chatty detail, inherited from her grandmother. The casserole was delicious. My attraction to thoughtful Mrs. Simmons—to both our disappointments—could not rise beyond the grandmother level.

From out of Unit 1033 launched Mrs. Farquer, a firecracker ex-attorney exactly my height who followed six newsfeeds though the day and let me know how all six were wrong. "Bullshit" was her word of choice. She wanted us to hook up, made no bones about that. I did try mixing our chemistry but nothing bubbled. The latest news about Mrs. Farquer is that she's back at the Mayo Clinic and won't return soon.

Mrs. Siebenbacher, in Unit 1200, the highest of our street numbers, had supple and gentle violinist's fingers with which she enjoyed holding one or both of my hands while in conversation. I enjoyed the holding myself. An ambulance came to retrieve her body on a Sunday morning—a sunny Sunday, as they tediously are in our section of the country— the ambulance understandably bringing with itself a general unease to our community. Gossip provided two versions for the cause of death. The first, chosen by many to believe, is that a congenital heart weakness mercifully caught up with poor Mrs. Siebenbacher. The second version blames an overdose of secobarbital.

Then, Miss Russetti, you appear at Casa del Sol, about six months back. Okay, why act a little dumb about the date. You arrived precisely five months and two weeks ago, because on that day, for the first time in my life, I began recording entries in what people call a diary. Let the soothsayers explain my motive to me.

* * * * *

From the start Miss Russetti you grabbed my attention, although not always for the most flattering of reasons. For instance you had stopped dyeing your hair without any attempt to hide the sharp line of color transition. The result is on the comical side, your hair resembling vanilla ice cream dipped into chocolate sauce, making a clumsy statement about the exit of the fake Used-to-Be and the emergence of the True You. But probably, like others among our neighbors, you just don't care anymore.

And apparently you've lost interest in wardrobe variety. What's your daily fascination with this ugly yellow top that might better fit a lumberjack? And returning to the topic of hair, I do detect it when you sometimes miss running a comb through those pillow twists before your morning walk in the communal flower garden.

However. None of these distractions allow me to ignore you, Miss Russetti—if only they would. Instead something is afoot here. Some potent power reels me into your vicinity without explanation. There is the simple stuff about you, such as the nice female cupping that still shapes the bottom of your bottom. (Sorry to cheapen myself by revealing my maleness, an old instinct stubbornly sputtering along down there with notions of its own.) There is the not-so-simple stuff, such as how in my mind those snarls in your hair only add another dash to the curls that nature gifted you, allowing a woman your age to keep the swirls and flips and pretty flounces of a girl. Finally what matters most is the totally not-simple thing: why I have an almost medical need to come close to you, very close, and learn your exact eye color.

To my regret we somehow missed the chance, in a formal fashion, to be introduced, Miss Russetti. So far, that is.

* * * * *

When you entered your courtyard condo those five months and two weeks ago immediately the dyslexic postwoman began delivering much of your mail (cottage #1101) with mine (cottage #1011). This nuisance made me grumpy at the start and you may have gotten a few crumpled letters from being shoved into your box. I cornered the postwoman, who religiously vowed to do better, but bless her, she failed, and before too long examining my mail for the presence of your mail was a bigger lift than the morning coffee. Please be assured I nowadays pass along your deliveries with appropriate respect and without delay. Yet I learn a lot on the fly while transferring an assortment of printed matter into the slot for #1101, and pleasing to me, we match each other in significant particulars. From alumni bulletins I find that we graduated the same year from the same respected midwestern university, where Miss (Ramona) Russetti must have sailed past me in a sea of 40,000 students, or was it merely 25,000 back in olden times. Our given and family names have the same double initials, RR, with the same number of syllables in each name—more confusion for unlucky Suzy, our letter carrier. We're not secretly married, are we? No, you specify a Miss for every address, almost proudly, with nary a Ms. to be found. I myself am a widower. A widower after thirteen years is also a type of Miss, especially if childless.

Your monthly statements from three brokerage firms and from three banks tell the world that you're a woman of financial substance. No surprise, for I understand fully the impressive cost of living in this retirement paradise, with its award-winning architecture and cadre of landscape crew, already expensive before any of the assistance charges a rapidly aging person may come to want or require. How did you earn your money? Several of your statements are addressed to Russetti Trust, suggesting you were born with the proverbial silver spoon in that untalkative mouth of yours. Or you could have been one of those Wall Street power players, back when you combed your hair better and still looked folks straight in the eye. Or maybe you raked in a fortune with a chain of Marijuana-for-Happy-Health boutiques. Studying you, I'm clueless. You amble and shuffle a bit on your rotations around the garden flowers these days, but those heels had to kick up, raise some dust and some hell, sometime, somewhere. Am I right?

Over the months no mail—that I could see—has come from the Department of Motor Vehicles, and your parking canopy stays empty. I might sell my car. Last trip out I got honked at, or I think so, for being slow at a green light. Who needs to put up with such insults. Perhaps you have the smarter idea, when you take the courtesy shuttle every Thursday and return with your groceries and other shopping. I should join you next Thursday, by sheer happenstance.

Also absent from my mailbox has been any personal letter or holiday card of yours addressed by a more energetic hand, written for example by a niece or nephew. This leads to the possibility we have another fact in common, as the only child in our families. And we both have nice teeth yet. Let's congratulate ourselves on that similarity at least.

* * * * *

Today the two of us approach the mailboxes in the lobby alcove, you slightly in advance. Our chance crossings in the lobby are infrequent because you pick up your mail on an erratic schedule, or really, no schedule. You wear your nauseous yellow top again, the one reminding me of dried mustard on a hot-dog bun. One sleeve is pushed up to an elbow while the other remains down at the wrist. Below the bottoms of your stretch pants and above the sockless athletic shoes, both darkish borders, glow six inches of dramatically pale skin. My tactic is to drift ever closer behind as you walk. The delicate rims of your ears, likewise pale, nudge themselves out through the swinging remnant strands of your bogus black hair.

At last comes another opportunity to confirm your eye color,

Miss Russetti. When you scan your mail, and wheel around, I can settle this issue. For months I had assumed that family name, its associated ethnicity, coupled with my sightings from afar, all added up to warm Mediterranean brown. Then you once slipped by, nearer, and I thought, Could those eyes be Tuscan slate gray?

I wait at the ready, your yellow shoulder insignificant inches from my chest, as you pop out your mail and toss the junk into the nearby waste receptacle, a sorting process you do with abandon. You turn. We actually collide. Through the wonder of bifocal lenses I focus down at the white crown of your head where the hair parts into a jaggedy path along its approximate center.

"Hello," I say as usual, avoiding any confrontational overtones.

"Hello," you repeat, also as usual. But bad luck. You neglect to lift your face, limiting my view to a quick downward closeup of a veil of eyelashes. Departing you trail a scent . . . familiar from my childhood. Aha, earlier that morning you must have miscalculated baking a batch of cookies and they came out burnt at the edges, creating an intriguing blend of smudge and sugar, too tasty not to eat.

Afterward I rummage through the trash bin and retrieve your discards, for taking home and reading at my leisure. Please take no offense, Miss Russetti. Most of your rejects duplicate my own mail, at any rate. There will be another Sunny Season Cruises brochure for retirees with time on their hands, money in their pockets, and a dreamy notion in their heads about a slow ship through tropical waters. There will be another solicitation for at least one of a variety of medical aids, including help for your vision, your hearing, your digestion, your joint pain, your sex life. Only the word *sex* won't be used, will it, Miss Russetti—substitute *romance* or *excitement*, accompanied by large illustrations of couples embracing, their smiles fixed in place, mature in age sure enough, but suspiciously more fit than we are. There could be my favorite advertisement, that four-fold flyer printed in dignified solemn greens, offering Pre-planned Final Services. I typically allot an extra minute trying to solve the difference between "pre-planned" and plain regular "planned." Feel free to draw me a diagram, using schoolbook syllogism circles if helpful, to knock the logic into my thick skull. The "final services" terminology I get, yes.

Now and again awaits an item of actual interest, to me, if not you, who did dump it into the trash. Those mailings from our college alma mater, for example, have enlightened me about my Miss Russetti. And today I fished out a legitimate financial statement complete with personal account number and tempting sums. You absolutely, positively should be more careful when flinging away mail by the handful. At my desk, having already slit open this envelope, I face a dilemma, and sense an opportunity. Instead of dropping this violated thing back into your mailbox, mysteriously patched with tape, I should properly return it in person, explaining, lamely, how I found it, why I opened it. The only tolerable part about lying in person to you is lying to you in person.

* * * * *

Here's what I plan to do. Here's my script for us, or according to our fuzzy-tongued mortuary friends, my "planned plan." Tomorrow while taking your morning spin through the garden, *poof,* I magically appear, initiate our customary "Hello" and when you attempt sidling past I block your path, which startles you, Miss Russetti, forcing your face up, revealing your naked eyes. Lonesome Brown? Dawn Gray, lit up like the promising hour before sunrise? To calm the scene I wave your misdirected envelope, rapidly detailing how we both are clients at the same firm (not true) and naturally how I had assumed it mine, had opened, had read, yack-yack-yack. You relax, and finally stopped, park a hand on a womanly hip. I continue with a further blur of details, about the amusing (not true) coincidence of our holding the very same securities (not true), and please follow down the list while I specify our wise selection of each bond, yack-yack-yack, my financial mumbo jumbo and cliches flying galore. Oh dear, you confess, your eyes of an indescribable color will need their reading glasses. And mine require their own bifocals, but having memorized the entire printed document I can pretend otherwise, if I wish. Damn me, I wish. You nod your head attentively as I ramble on. Generously, you compliment my eyesight. I compliment your mustard sweater. No use to stop the lying once lying is successfully underway. Soon you invite me back to your home for your reading glasses and tea. Inside the kitchen clings the aroma of scorched cookies, just as I had suspected and hoped.

So, no, no, Miss Russetti, this plan I pre-planned never had its chance to happen, did it. We never had tea together, did we. While shaving in preparation for our garden rendezvous I gave myself a nasty slash, blood everywhere, a major repair job required on my chin, and a wounded spectacle too embarrassing to share with the public, particularly you. I had no intention of sporting a big fat bandage that shouted out how this vain geezer tried to look like a courting Casanova again.

* * * * *

My persistence amazes me, because away I go into the courtyard garden this morning, for real. An intervening week has allowed the angry gash on my chin to quiet down, although unfortunately, every delay turns justifying your opened envelope into a stiffer challenge. But I intend to try/ to lie, even if my nervous misbehaving heartbeat doesn't approve.

What specimens have we here, displayed among this rainbow of different flowers. Other than roses I can identify next to nothing. My wife gave up holding a normal conversation about flowers with me, simplified it all instead by saying "the pink ones" or "the purple ones." Where are you hiding today, Miss Russetti, when I could use a hand with these botanical names, and in the bargain, why not the hand itself. Apparently you skedaddled off into town and we must postpone our introduction. Again. For some reason I'm breathing a huge sigh of relief. For another reason I'm hardly breathing. For every convoluted reason this pursuit is turning into work. Anyhow, my marred chin gets another day to heal.

My return walk wends its pleasant way in sunshine through the extensive garden, technically four themed gardens in a staggered sequence the manager has informed me, one theme being roses, thankfully. Your condo cottage #1101 fronts a theme patterned with lots of desert rock, sized from lava boulders to dry creek-bed gravel. Already from a distance I notice that the blinds of your patio glass door, at your private terrace entrance, have been left open, letting in morning sun. It takes a lost or devious hiker over eighty meandering footsteps—I lost count near the end—to angle across that faux Mojave and end smack dab at your home. Now add my peeking at your furniture to peeking at your mail—and call it romance, call it criminal. I swear, the briefest peek and away I would scoot like a good boy, except my lord, the sunlight entering the room hits a photograph of Miss Russetti so perfectly, so very bright and concentrated, it might as well be a lightning bolt that refuses to disappear after the flash.

Edging up to the glass I stomp on a cluster of (nameless) flowers, another apology for later. My feet go astray because my eyes never leave the picture. You know which picture, Miss Russetti. Of almost poster dimensions, expensively framed in metal, professionally photographed, it hangs center stage on the wall over the cream leather sofa: a father, a mother, a curly black-haired daughter. That defiant tousle of inky hair gives you away instantly, Miss Russetti.

Much in your family portrait I recognize, including social confidence likely backed by a fancy education, by financial heft, by emotional equipoise, or an excellent imitation of these. Also I can trace the genetic shape of the daughter's temples and elevated cheekbones back to the father, her eyebrow arc and elegant jawline to the mother, her facial balance to both. I locate the family trait of a contained smile, suitable in this case for a formal studio study. What catches me off guard, Miss Russetti, is you, with your lurking violent beauty.

I have to gawk. Are you 17 or 27? Because you represent bud and bloom combined. In the youthful blank purity of your face I see a future still unfolded, with a tenderness easily bruised if not later coaxed, patiently, into the fullness of experience. Yet I see those lips of yours, already as sensuous, provocative even, as any temptress could put to use. And your neck. And your blouse. Your blouse is open two buttons down, the exposed throat a kind of invitation, a loop of matched pearls caressing your collarbone, altogether enough to make a man jealous of a piece of inanimate jewelry. Steady as your Russetti expression tries to be, a wild energy escapes out in a human force field, jumps along the many irrepressible tips of your hair, sparkles in your eyelashes, fires your complexion, practically fogs inside the picture frame with hot breath. I must repeat, you're spectacular, Miss Russetti.

I'm curious. How long did you stand there, in the room, in the flesh, by the cream sofa, before I notice you looking out at me looking in at you, or rather at a photograph of you? Minutes, surely.

We both must wonder why I don't throw a cheery wave ("Hello!"), don't blush, don't flinch. I don't because I can't. Directly in front of me is everything about you, if I can decipher it, both the Miss Russetti up there on the wall and the Miss Russetti here standing on the floor, side-by-side, before-and-after, the saga of a life. Bloodless paper or not, that immobilized image of young Ramona Russetti makes you more alive to me than ever before, no matter how many daily glimpses of you in motion in your mustardy yellow sweater.

First I have the nerve to check for your eye color, but the pair of you, photograph and woman, are just beyond range, and I continue on, comparing Miss Russetti to Miss Russetti. Do you look old enough to be the mother of yourself? Yes, and older, as you in life are older than your own parents in the picture. Nevertheless I understand exactly where you fit, whether on the wall or in the room, because you are no latter-day corrupted version of the wonderful Miss Russetti with her string of pearls. There is one Miss Russetti only.

Please tell me the stories. I want to know. There must

be stories. Who, or what, did you ignite with that throttled urgency of yours when it finally broke loose, and before its flame blew out. Were there ambitions, grand or modest. I want to know how much smiling you learned to do. For the record, neither of us breaks the bank with smiles around here. I want to know whether you cried, and why. I want to know how you sleep at night, whether in peace or restless, whether dreaming, or to escape dreams, whether curled up tight or sprawled and vulnerable.

I want to know if you always slept alone. Agreed, agreed, agreed, that's none of my business, except for my wanting to know. I look at your lips, back then, or at this moment, and believe it inconceivable they went unkissed. And certainly, without doubt, over the years, hopelessly seduced fingers have yearned to explore the dark thicket of your hair, yearned to wander the maze of those whorls, before arriving, touching, at the smoothness of your neck, seeking there that soft pocket on your throat where your pulse beats faster and faster. Did you let any fingers take that trip. Did anybody ever spout a gush of sentences like mine solely for you. Have you had lovers. I hope so, I do. More importantly, have you had love. Hold on . . . hold on . . . are these sticky tears gumming up my eyesight?

At this juncture you leave the room. Likely to telephone security.

* * * * *

This is no longer a game, is it, Miss Russetti. I spilled a smelly pot of goofiness all over us. Good, let me clean up the stink.

I sit here tonight at my desk, cataloging the coming day and what I must do. Upon waking I'll swing my legs over the left side of the bed, pushing my feet into house slippers called California Comfort but manufactured in Sri Lanka. Next will come a dozen sliding steps to the bathroom where the toilet seat is already raised, from using it twice since midnight. At the sink will follow two pumps from the soap dispenser, two splashes of cold water across each closed eye, two blots from a cheerful orange towel that I might put in the laundry this week. Another dozen slipper slides will take me back to the closet where I put on whatever hangs near the front, thereby avoiding a tangle of clothes hangers, or worse, a tangle of choices. Onward another dozen slipper slides for breakfast, which will be either classic granola cereal or classic granola with almonds, a third of a bowl in acidophilus milk. Another dozen, plus another dozen, slides, still in slippers, back to the bathroom again, squeezing a smidgen less than an inch of mint toothpaste onto a toothbrush overdue for replacement. I'll wet down my hair as the faucet runs. While I could shave at this station on the timeline, a later day is probably soon enough, when I can handle the whole maintenance process in one efficient effort—shaving, earwax removal, trimming nose and ear hairs, clipping nails. Again a dozen of those slipper slides back to the bedroom.

In the bureau drawer unfailingly wait matched socks, since I solved that problem ages ago by buying multiple packages of the identical patternless color.

My routine will be great comfort to me, unlike the nagging restlessness and outright recklessness of my recent weeks. And yet a final chore of leftover business remains. Tomorrow morning, promptly after tying my shoes, I must return to cottage #1101 again, for a last visit, Miss Russetti.

Your ancient envelope, showing wear, I'll deliver in person, placing it on your doorstep, not in your mailbox, because I don't intend to behave like a complete coward. Don't worry, Miss Russetti, I'm through with fantasies, done with charades. No more asinine lies, and actually, no talking, period. On your letter I already wrote boldly with my best block print: **FOUND THIS IN THE PAPER TRASH. SORRY ABOUT OPENING IT. SORRY FOR BEING TOO CURIOUS ABOUT YOU.**

* * * * *

Either you spotted me coming along my way, or you have the instincts of a lioness at her lair: whichever, there you are, erect and ready behind your window, watching. I deserve no less. Punishment should be public.

I lean the envelope against the doorsill, bracing for your reaction to another presumptuous act. The reaction? None. Miss Russetti, you show zero interest in that sad abused stick of paper, your eyes never shifting from mine, looking without betraying why you look. If you must stand like a statue, let it be a shape frozen with scorn, or any other recognizable emotion. I demand some sign that acknowledges the fuss and bother I caused you, a minimal signal at least, any fleeting scowl or quizzical squint. But zero. Instead your watching, by itself, seems to represent the full available effort you care to spend on miserable me. Rather than a fireworks finale, my presence here counts for scant more nuisance than the snags that disrupt your hair most mornings.

No use in my having another go at your eye color, Miss Russetti. Once upon a time that would have been the prize for getting closer to you. Once upon a time. What a dangerously addictive expression of possibilities for us. Miss Russetti, once upon a time, with our twin initials, RR, we could have founded a new railroad company together. Once upon a time our same initials could have stood for our same name and the mail in the same mailbox would always be ours. Get it, Miss Russetti? Once upon a time we could have insulted each other daily and flown hand-in-hand to the stars daily, and ultimately, taken the bus together to the mall every Thursday. The point is, once upon a time, Ramona, we would have had a Once Upon a Time.

We didn't and here we stand, two senior citizens looking at each other with only the Time part of Once Upon. Compounding the short calendar we live in, I already used up my enthusiasm for my own Mr. RR, as you have for your Miss RR. Ramona, so you'll know, as a matter of clarification, my hope for us had been we could strike a possible deal. Seems that I'm just tired of the old me, not of the old you. To me you're still new. My idea was we could make a switch or a trade and exchange interest in each other. My idea was that we two aren't way down at the end of the Big Show yet, maybe more someplace in the middle of the end.

Keep on staring, sweet statue, because I see now what you see, what people mean by saying an old fool is the worst of fools. For weary us, wisdom is discovering when to rest. I thank heaven for your favor, Ramona, of not allowing our comedy to expand into exhausting hurtful farce. Away I vanish, returning to my #1011, you there behind inside your #1101, two separate threads of a tale, left at peace, unwoven, untold.

* * * * *

The very next Thursday a persistent social buzz outside brings me to my window. I find you, Miss Russetti, in conversation with the beanpole Mrs. Wilson of cottage #1088, waiting for the shuttle. Your voice is louder than I ever heard. When the van arrives Mrs. Wilson hustles off, over her shoulder urging you to catch up. The van driver toots his horn. Miss Russetti, before following you pause twice—definitely twice—to peer into *my* window. Your hair has been chopped short, all brilliant silver. You wear a sweater I never saw before, fuchsia possibly. The question is now, what do I make of this, and you, if anything.

Anything.

Kisses at the Beach

1.

The principal candidates for drowning on Sunday are four.

Clarissa Kreshmeyer

At age 22, Clarissa has completed the best month of her life, during which she may have smiled more than any other person in all of San Mateo County, California. She has lost those last three pounds and is now certifiably slim. She is now a college graduate. She is now engaged to a man who actually does make her heart throb, their wedding set for September—a date removed enough to enjoy anticipation, close enough for immediate excitement.

Last Friday a large flattering photograph of her already pretty face appeared on the *Burlingame Journal* social page. "Clarissa Kreshmeyer . . . her recent baccalaureate in . . . a life-long resident of . . . has announced . . . to Richard Holland, Jr." The Kreshmeyer family has bought and scissored six newspaper copies, four clippings preserved for albums, another being mailed off to the Hollands near Syracuse, New York, and one pinned by Clarissa beside a mirror in her room. There, she can see the photograph, read those words, confirm them by checking the pleased image in the mirror. "Mrs. Clarissa Holland," she occasionally tests aloud, to savor the euphony, teasing her parents about the improvement over her birth name, with its slur of k's, r's and s's that had tangled many a tongue over the years, her own included.

Richard Holland, Jr.

Called "Richie" by his fiancée, even if nobody had before, he is more than happy that Clarissa began it, due to a clumsy confusion among the Hollands themselves, caused when distinguishing "Tall Richard" the father from "Small Richard" the son. In time Tall/Small literally grew nonsensical, as 6' 6" Richard, Jr. left New York five years ago to play basketball at a California college. During that period three colleges were attended, less and less basketball played. While he did have his share of fun in the California sun, a haze of indirection plagued him, and his field of academic study ricocheted from Sport Kinesiology to Theater Arts to something known as

Recreational Services. Richard has never failed a class and needs, he judges, "only about one more year to wind matters up." His romances—before Clarissa—had tended toward girls with plenty of hair who wore bold eye shadow and were skillful laughers. If asked, he could recall their names, probably not in correct sequence.

Richard met Clarissa at a campus dance, hardly a year ago: he arriving with one of the aforementioned laughers, she with a pleasant Somebody. At evening's end, they properly left the dance in the company of their original partners, although both, already disloyal, awaited a promised telephone call. Shortly afterward Richard found his life easing into the secure harbor, the protective attentions, of sweet Clarissa Kreshmeyer. Daily he thanks his lucky stars for his fine fortune. Daily he soaks up this unfamiliar relaxation. Unlike with his other young women, it impresses him how Clarissa seems more attractive the longer he knows her, and more attractive, rather than less, when he catches her not wearing cosmetics. Richard has firmly tucked Clarissa into his marital pocket and intends that she never falls out.

Mrs. Kreshmeyer

She thinks her daughter made a "good catch," despite silently believing, as a cautious mother hen does, that as a general rule it is wise to place the wedding an extra six months down the calendar, in case minds should change. There are far too many divorces nowadays, are there not? Her own sister has had two. But Richard does present an excellent picture, being tall, strappingly athletic, and handsome in a way she always favored, namely, like a 1940s Hollywood leading man, with a strong jawline and straight white teeth. And Richard is *nice*, unfailingly mild-natured and polite. Courtesy counts for a lot in Mrs. Kreshmeyer's mind. Although curious about the Hollands way out east, she has merely heard that Mrs. Holland's health is not the best and that Mr. Holland "took an early retirement." Clarissa herself could not fill in the specifics, which might raise eyebrows in suspicious quarters, yet this partial information—its multiple suggestions, mostly melancholy—evokes in Clarissa's mother an inchoate sympathy toward her future son-in-law.

Mrs. Kreshmeyer's favorite remembrance of Clarissa recalls a plump obedient child with umpteen dollars' worth of braces on her teeth. Ah, mother and daughter throughout those years had spent hours of chatty companionship together on after-school afternoons and on quiet evenings when the boisterous older brothers were out of the home. Eventually the orthodontics had vanished. That persistent chubbiness, once practically yielded to as an expectation, came more under control, until of late it had disappeared as totally as those glaring braces. Mrs. Kreshmeyer hopes Clarissa's weight will stay down, unlike another former shapely bride she knows well.

Mr. Kreshmeyer

He feels no special enthusiasm for Richard Holland, Jr.

No doubt this is inevitable, with a father and his only girl, and youngest, fondest child. In his living room he has watched Clarissa and her chosen man cozy up, planning their September, a sight that caused a nagging in his memory, resurrecting ghosts of phrases read many yesteryears ago, in some obligatory college course. What were the words? They were from a poem, that he remembered, because he had read so few of those in his lifetime, all at school. Stored up in the garage attic, for reasons of compulsive Kreshmeyer thrift, was every old magazine subscription and textbook the family had ever possessed, and Mr. Kreshmeyer just could not resist the search. In the dim attic he had pawed through the paper heap until he found his poem, aided by a flashlight's moody beam:

> *Let your father fret*
> *over you becoming red meat:*
> *torn raggedy and swallowed by*
> *a canine cavalier pulling you off*
> *under his own bush*
> *for his permanent bone.*

Mr. Kreshmeyer had smiled broadly in appreciation of his successful memory and of the father's words themselves. Moving his flashlight down, the lines continued, "Better to get devoured you say/ than go rancid, unused, since/ that's the purpose of meat," whereupon he had closed the book with a nasty clap. Here was exactly why not to read poems. They have a habit of spoiling things by churning one idea into another then off into another—it gave him a headache. No, a pain in the ass to be anatomically truthful.

Overall the progress of his family does not match what Mr. Kreshmeyer had once imagined. One unmarried son, currently stationed in Alabama, a state Mr. Kreshmeyer can scarcely particularize on any mental map, is a lieutenant in the Army, although he never played with toy soldiers or guns as a boy. The other son, also unmarried, and a stockbroker trainee living in Van Nuys, southern California, has never saved (hence never invested) a nickel his entire life long. Both boys, therefore, are an expanding puzzle to their father, and given the infrequency of their visits, increasingly remote. Neither son indicates the slightest interest in the father's insurance agency, a business Mr. Kreshmeyer has built into a real money-maker over the past twenty years of devoted labor. He supposes that this Richie is now his main chance for a business associate, subsequently a partner, ultimately his successor. Already there has been around-the-edges chat about whether Richard should bother to finish college. Soon they would, point-blank, request Mr. Kreshmeyer's advice. What if he shocked their socks off by saying: "I'm like a poem. I don't have any straight answers about anything."

2.

Sunday, 10:30 *ante meridian.* The Kreshmeyers' flawlessly clean, black Mercedes SUV is packed with picnic supplies and beach gear. A low fog looks serious, like it intends to linger for the day, but these social outings, once underway, seldom lose critical momentum. As an insurance man, Mr. Kreshmeyer inspects the tires, which he has made certain will be Michelin with an extra ply in the sidewalls. Richard sits in front beside the father, as mother and daughter pair up behind.

Their route spans the narrow San Francisco peninsula, from the inner shoreline across the coastal hills to the Pacific and a sweep of ocean called Half Moon Bay. The unannounced yet obvious purpose of the trip—planned by Clarissa and her mother—is to practice being a family. With the Kreshmeyer-Holland future being launched inside this solemnly black Mercedes, the weight of such an important venture bears down, and conversational efforts suffer at the start. Luckily, banalities construct a sort of comfort ladder, each exchange about the weather another step where meaningful talk seems less and less a requirement, until a step on the ladder can be reached where silence is not a failure.

In this quiet Mrs. Kreshmeyer begins to think, as she does of late, about her only niece—her older sister's daughter— who at twenty-six is already stuck in the muck of a divorce. The sister, without any transition whatsoever, had erupted into throttled sobs while announcing the news over the phone, leaving Mrs. Kreshmeyer shaken, because her sister never cried. Well, way, way back, there had been that miserable tenth birthday when the sister's presents got misplaced in the wrong car trunk. But those had been plain tears. What

Mrs. Kreshmeyer heard on the phone was violent. Instead of emotion, the noises sounded more like a companion sitting at your restaurant table (which did happen once for Mrs. Kreshmeyer) who in the middle of a little gossip commences to strangle on a deadly lump of chicken gristle. Mrs. Kreshmeyer wonders if her sister's own two failed marriages are what torture her so, and how very terrible to infect your daughter's life, the same as passing on a cancer gene. She casts a sidling look at Clarissa. "Did you bring a coat?"

Clarissa answers with an indulgent smile. "I believe *you* sneaked in my heavy Navy coat, the one I haven't worn in about three years."

"Did I?" Mrs. Kreshmeyer switches directions to the back of Richard's head, whose hair is thick and lengthy enough to allow a hint of curls. How many men can you love and leave, Mrs. Kreshmeyer might ask her sister, or who will leave you. If more than one, is two the limit? If more than two, why not twenty?

Not remarkably, Clarissa also is examining the back of Richard's hair. For although the scenery outside has turned sylvan with a luscious wall of evergreens, nonetheless, she will look at what attracts her the most. She has put her lips on that cushiony hair a thousand times, almost, its taste and manly smell exotically different from her female world. Admittedly, Richie's hair could eventually thin like her father's, who reveals from this rear angle as much scalp as hair. "And it won't matter to me one single bit!" Clarissa nearly proclaims aloud.

Completing the family's unity of focus, Mr. Kreshmeyer, too, is comparing himself to Richard, a contrast hard to avoid with his future son-in-law close by, in a matching position and seat, looming there really, all six-and-a-half feet of him or eight feet, or whatever height it took to scrape your hair on the car's headliner and soil it. Mr. Kreshmeyer on his part measured 5' 9" at his last annual physical, or "nearly" the nurse had appended. Early in his faraway high-school days he had tried out for the baseball team and got dumped at the first tryout practice, an episode that ended sports for him. Possibly with a body like Richard's here, he would have found success, possibly not.

Not that Mr. Kreshmeyer qualifies as a superstar talent at his job either. For a salesman, he has no exceptional skills as a smooth talker, and he could never duplicate his ex-colleague Edwin Mackle's whoop-tee-do method of packing hotel conference rooms with "seminars" on "risk-management theory," and from the podium, by the force of a golden tongue, sign a slew of fresh accounts. Mr. Kreshmeyer's style is without showmanship. He spends hours scratching and scratching for his clients, until he comes up with the cheapest policies with the fullest coverage. He always keeps his appointments. He always returns his calls. Clients rarely leave him. When he opened his own agency forward progress had been glacially slow before relentlessly increasing, a jot bigger and a jot bigger yet, and in another glacier parallel, a layer added to weighty layer, with more clients spreading a good word to their friends.

On the last Sunday of every month Mr. Kreshmeyer retires to his home study with a lime soda and updates his personal financial holdings. The family, should they pass by, can hear him slurping in slow satisfaction, but the soda is not the tastiest part. He sums up the latest price quotes for his stock-and-bond portfolio. He adds the current interest to his bank accounts. He calculates the month's profit from the agency and reviews the value of all real estate. Finally, comes the grand total: a number significant enough to forget about finishing his soda.

Mr. Kreshmeyer does not inform his family they have a boatload of money. Although the amount is a pleasure, or sometimes an excitement, he never decides what it proves, if anything, other than he can buy expensive cars. No money would ever make him taller than (almost) 5' 9". If he tried out for a baseball team again, Mr. Kreshmeyer would still do no better than hit one loopy foul ball for six pitches, as happened his sophomore year in high school.

Outside, the lowered sky melds into forest, where hillsides of redwoods crowd upward to the crest of the Santa Cruz Mountains. Inside the warm Mercedes a lullaby lull takes hold. The engine hums its steady tune, tires on pavement singing in harmony.

There must have been trips of his own, imagines Richard, with sensations like these, his head leaned against the window, a gentle buzz from the roadway conducting from tire to glass to temple, as he drowsily let himself be carried somewhere toward a destination. As an only child, he must have had these moments of blind trust. One photograph, at least, shows him sitting in a boxy Chevrolet sedan, his mother behind the wheel, apparently about to drive away. Both of them are grinning their goodbyes up at the camera. He sits the lowest, still a Small Richard. His mother displays those key attributes she has bequeathed her son: lanky body, coils of summer-streaked brown hair, a sparkle in the almost-onyx eyes, the generous mouth with symmetrically ideal teeth. That picture was taken about ten months before her impossible backyard accident, when his mother lost those front teeth and one of those lovely dark eyes. The left.

Crossing the summit, the Mercedes follows curves down the coastal slope, into westward vistas, the forest interrupted now by upland pastures. With a visual *voilà*, the Pacific abruptly shows itself below, revealing the outline of Half Moon Bay—a shape, accurately observed, closer to a crescent moon, thus allowing in stronger forces from the open sea and limiting its usefulness as a port.

They park near the water to evaluate what awaits them at the beach. Despite the fog having elevated, Mrs. Kreshmeyer locates above merely two or three patches of pallid blue forcing their color into sight, and a stout breeze ruffles the ocean swells. "Whitecaps," Mr. Kreshmeyer says, and he and Mrs. Kreshmeyer suggest diverting the trip to Golden Gate

Park, in San Francisco, where indoor options were possible with their picnic, such as a museum or an aquarium.

"But we did plan it all for here," Clarissa says, with disappointment at the ready in her face.

Therefore Richard supports his Clarissa and everybody loads up with baskets and collapsible chairs, locking the Mercedes, Mr. Kreshmeyer reviewing every door and window before they trudge off through the sand. Clarissa, in snug jeans and a baggy sweatshirt with her college logo across the front, is barefoot, her toes squiggling in the softness at each bouncy step. At her side Richard has on a jogging suit and low-profile trainers, minus socks, ambling with that loosey-goosey grace the way skilled athletes do. Mrs. Kreshmeyer wears sandals, sensible twill slacks, full-length sleeves, a scarf, an extra sweater folded over her arm. And Mr. Kreshmeyer is a fashion and seaside debacle: carmine golfing cap, orange windbreaker over a dress shirt, beige corduroy pants, black street shoes (already collecting sand).

Against the shelter of a small dune, facing the ocean, they put down the food, spread out the blankets and unfold the chairs, settling in for their afternoon. In front of them noisy waves roil the water and scoot fans of gritty foam along the shore, sandpipers scampering in an ensemble, on the lookout for morsels. Off at the horizon several fishing boats carry on their work. Overhead, sharp against the muddled sky, dozens of snowy gulls glide and plunge in a blend of collective and chaotic paths. All considered, the picnic site provides an excellent panorama of Half Moon Bay, with its hills and scattered buildings in the background. On the beach the tourist population is spotty for a Sunday. Nearest the Kreshmeyers sits a tight circle of three young couples, evidently on a beachcomber outing, or a date, since they have a harvest of flotsam piled there, and now are drinking beer, too rapidly, and laughing, too loudly. "Just our luck," groans Mr. Kreshmeyer. He predicts, "Bet you some serious money they'll litter those beer cans."

This beach is noteworthy for two features, the first being the quality of its driftwood specimens, wonderful redwood pieces washed down mountain creeks and polished in the surf by winter storms, and the second being drownings, an average of 1.7 fatalities per year, according to official California statistics.

3.

Normally Clarissa Kreshmeyer is a direct person without any ornamentation to her manners or motives. Last semester a professor had complimented her—she never figured out quite how—by describing her as "a sans-serif sort of gal." Except today Clarissa yields to a forgivable vanity. The sun may be absent, the wind unfriendly, the water downright chilly, yet Clarissa announces she intends to take a swim. What she intends, factually, is to have her new body seen in her new bathing suit. She deserves this small prideful wish, having clearly earned it.

"Why, you'll freeze!" protests Mr. Kreshmeyer, about to scold her, until he remembers that he quit scolding his daughter a decade ago.

Standing, Clarissa peels the jeans down, down, down, shimmying hips, an unintended seductive dance that jolts her parents, and oh yes, at least one of the neighboring young men is following the action. Off comes Clarissa's sweatshirt. Her bikini (Sensuous Silver, to believe the manufacturer) dazzles brighter than the whitest seagull flying above, and she looks delectable, every goose bump of her.

"Here I go," announces Clarissa.

"Brave girl," calls Richard.

Mrs. Kreshmeyer readies two fluffy bath towels.

Clarissa trots toward the water with her ponytail swishing, dry sand jumping from under her heels, and now definitely all three of the nearby young men are watching this silver maiden pass. Reaching the surf Clarissa enacts a traditional playlet, the one where, toe testing the water, at the cold shock the swimmer hops a retreat from the ocean's surge. But Clarissa is here in her $93.00 swimsuit, knows what she needs to do, and with resolve she splashes forward and half-trips, half-dives, into the Pacific.

Popping up, sputtering, Clarissa tosses her wet hair back and wades into deeper water where she can swim. She ducks to let a wave roll overhead and after, bobbing, strokes out past the jumble of the shorebreak, using a precise, daintily correct

Australian crawl learned from childhood YWCA lessons, appearing to move with minimal effort. Better yet, Clarissa senses that her body, with a previously undiscovered talent, is traveling without the bother of much leg kick.

Up on the beach Mrs. Kreshmeyer already frets. "For goodness' sake, why does she go out that far?"

"Great swimmer," says Richard, identifying one more virtue about his Mrs. Holland-to-be.

Mr. Kreshmeyer agrees. "Look at her zip along."

Clarissa, meanwhile, is centered in a narrow band of darker, murkier water, a dirty line pointing out from shore, filled with choppy peaks. She has stopped swimming altogether yet continues briskly seaward.

"Maybe so," sighs Mrs. Kreshmeyer, "but why that far out?"

Noticing the beach grow distant, Clarissa turns around and digs hard with her arms. She works for ten vigorous minutes, cycling those arms, whipping her locked legs. To maintain a steady presto rhythm she chants to herself: *Time to get back, time to get back, get back, get back.*

"Fine," says Mrs. Kreshmeyer, "okay, she's headed in, finally. We can start lunch now."

A peeled egg each. With the boiled eggs went salt and pepper, and a shaker of paprika for anyone wanting a piquant accent. Three flavors of potato chips get fetched out immediately, Classic Ruffles, Hawaiian BBQ, Sour Cream & Chives, because Mr. Kreshmeyer has a weakness for chips.

In a case of overkill, Mrs. Kreshmeyer brought along a bag of honey-coated popcorn "for munching." Richard takes a handful. Another extra is cold pizza, some slices for the hardy appetite with fat chunks of ham and pineapple, some slices for the healthy-minded with tomatoes, peppers, mushrooms, artichokes, onions, olives. In the ice chest wait bottles of spring water, cranapple juice, lemonade, diet Pepsi. "Choices, choices . . ." moans a delighted Richard.

After the ten minutes Clarissa has gotten nowhere, and pausing, and panting, she cannot deny that the faraway figures of her parents and Richie are smaller than before. Her exertion should have Clarissa in a sweat, but she feels colder, very cold. "Dear god," she realizes, "this must be . . . a what . . . a riptide. I'm caught in a riptide." And a riptide it is, or rip current, by either name a vicious river running inside its own ocean, and counter-directional, caused in part by an invisible chute sluicing the water rearward with sufficient power to suck sand, and anything else, out to sea. Clarissa shivers with disappointment and shame. She must not, will not, frighten her family or spoil this day, and pushing the wet unraveled hair from the circular edges of her face, Clarissa commits herself to utter determination, lashing toward shore again.

"Let me explain the sandwich fixings," says Mrs. Kreshmeyer, the Tupperware arranged around her like ranks of soldiers poised for action. "The roast beef and turkey meats are in these. Use separately, or mix, Richard, whatever you wish. Over here are four cheeses. Jack. Swiss. Provolone.

Sharp cheddar. Use separately or mix. Here in this bigger one is Romaine lettuce. Here, side-by-side, are the pickles, dill and sweet. Next is red onions, very mild. The mayo is right here in front. The regular mustard and horseradish over there. For breads we have sourdough or wheat rolls or these croissants."

Mr. Kreshmeyer, nibbling his third variety of chip, declares his wife "a genius with a picnic."

"Clarissa better hurry in," says Richard, "or this feast will be gone, that's how hungry I am." He stands and beckons with an exaggerated sweep of his arm. "Does she see me?"

Mrs. Kreshmeyer positions the towels closer at hand. "Why the girl wants to suffer, I don't know, certainly." To hide the peevishness, she speaks with a mouthful of croissant.

Mr. Kreshmeyer, who has assembled a monster sandwich, takes a messy bite, squints seaward. "She's waving back."

Sloshing about, athwart the riffle ridge where choppiness slaps at the sides of her head, Clarissa tries to float, spitting water, her heart knocking from the pointless struggle. She is reduced to a stage beyond tiredness, begs herself to rest, wants to widen her mouth and pull more air inside, more energy, but her stomach retches from the brine. The more she twists in despair, the more her legs keep dropping, two foolish anchors that threaten to take their own ship under. Uninvited, the thought *goodbye* finds its poisonous way into Clarissa's defenseless mind.

After eating a complete corner off his sandwich, Mr. Kreshmeyer asks, "Is she talking to herself?"

Mrs. Kreshmeyer permits her irritation and her voice to rise. "I don't like Clarissa in that water. I don't." To distract what she mistakes for anger, she turns to the outside row of plastic food containers. "Let's leave room for dessert. This one is my custard. I sprinkled it with cinnamon."

"Wave her in again," Mr. Kreshmeyer tells Richard.

Richard, for the moment, does not find her.

"This one is the brownies. They're a couple of days old so try them with the custard if they seem dry. This one is the peach pie."

"I can't see her," says Mr. Kreshmeyer. He puts down his sandwich.

"The whipped cream in still in the cooler. There's a big tub. Use some on the pie, or with the brownies could be a good idea, an excellent idea."

Richard points. "Over there. That bobbing head over there."

"Also in the yellow cooler . . . also in the cooler . . ."

"Listen," says Mr. Kreshmeyer, cupping a hand to his ear.

What they hear is a thin squeaking, not much louder than the onshore wind, reminiscent perhaps of a kitten, mewing, lost in an overgrown field.

Mrs. Kreshmeyer takes in an unplanned breath. "Richard, is she calling your name? Something's wrong. Is something wrong?"

Clarissa's father is on his feet, stringing together words. "No, no, no, no, no. Look at her head, look there, look. Go after her, go, go, quick, quick, quick!"

Spilling one of her desserts—the peach pie—Mrs. Kreshmeyer is also on her feet, by her husband. "Richard, is she *sinking*? Richard!"

Now Mr. Kreshmeyer is away running, shedding his windbreaker, shaking the stubborn thing off the last arm, and he heads into the surf, thrashing forward as the ocean rises to his waist, his chest, his neck. With a helpful tug the riptide guides Mr. Kreshmeyer into its deeper channel. Drifting sand fills those street shoes to the top and his corduroy pants wrap, menacingly, around his legs. Even by walking on his toes, with water lapping at his tipped chin, 5' 9" Mr. Kreshmeyer no longer can spot Clarissa on the other side of the swells, and for this reason alone he refuses to fight the current carrying him outward to his only daughter.

Richard and Mrs. Kreshmeyer stand together, sea froth around their ankles. She pleads in a mangled soliloquy to the world, a wail so squashed out of shape it might as well be a foreign language. Was she saying "He shouldn't go farther in," or was it "He can't even swim"? Whichever, Richard pays her no interest. He is the opposite of Mrs. Kreshmeyer's agitation. Out in front of him Clarissa Kreshmeyer and her father are vanishing from the mortal earth, and Richard watches like today is just what happens on Sundays when you take your sweetheart to the beach.

Of course Clarissa will drown. He loves her, and of course she will drown. Why deny the idea. It was Sunday once before, after all, when an event occurred more unusual than this Sunday now, noteworthy enough to get reported in every newspaper in the state of New York, including *The Times*. The weather on that other Sunday, furthermore, was friendlier than today, with only stray clouds in a sunny sky, with a heavy summer warmth instead of this foggy chill, with a lush green lawn to walk across instead of this gray and littered sand. And instead of a giant sullen ocean yanking away a wonderful girl, on that earlier Sunday an unseen sliver of nature struck down a wonderful mother—a slight-of-hand trick so unique it exists, in most minds, as a fanciful idiom about striking twice, or some harmless statistic hidden in almanacs.

Richard is not surprised here today at Half Moon Bay. Surprised is when your mother, being the unfortunate taller of you two, gasps from an invisible blow and is flung into a limp human heap in the middle of your own lawn. Surprised is thinking you heard no thunder, unless that awful gasp was the actual thunder. Surprised is never recognizing your mother's face again—regardless of those brutal surgeries with their unbearable price of pain and lost hopes—until finally you take her different face and name it Mother. Surprised is reading and later rereading the truncated news accounts about the "miracle survivor." In no form did Richard ever discover the miracle part. What he saw was his mother retreating more and more into her bedroom, seldom seen anywhere in any season without her opaque sunglasses, and, it developed, seldom seen period.

Off in her lonely solitude Clarissa has been crying, salt

scalding her eyes into pink tears. There is much to cry about: the iciness, the cruel fatigue, the cramps tormenting her body, and most of all, her regrets over losing this September and the anniversaries of more Septembers.

"Am I already dying?" wonders Clarissa, unable to register when her face is above or below the surface, snuffling saltwater into her nostrils, which spreads fiery torture along the full surface of her skull. She swallows a large gulp of ocean. She vomits underwater. Her throat and lungs convulse in reflexive indecision, desperate to drag in oxygen, desperate to shut out the killing fluid. Clarissa perceives intense darkness and a counterpoint flood of light, a momentous, celestial pattern that repeats itself to reiterate its importance. The watery embrace squeezes her, insists, insists, and recognizing the logic, Clarissa consents to end the agony.

Half Moon Bay is about to factor in fatality number 2 for the present year, thereby bumping up its 1.7 annual average.

4.

Plop, down go the beer cans, not yet empty, good beer gurgling into the sand, as the three noisy young men race unsmiling to the cold Pacific, diving in without a hint of hesitation. Soon two of them are latching onto Mr. Kreshmeyer's submerged shirt, under the armpits, and in unison they tug him back to land, where he wobbles, with his dripping, sorry clothes and his sorrowful face. The three waiting girls cluster around Mr. Kreshmeyer, draping a blanket across his shaky shoulders, and every head turns to watch the third rescuer.

Riding the riptide for speed the young man reaches Clarissa blazingly fast, and without pause or gentleness he snags his fingers into her hair, jerking her aloft, like a puppeteer pulling a lifeless doll up on stage, and mightily he raises and flips her, to pour water from her mouth, with two fingers hooking phlegm out of the throat. Those same fingers press the carotid artery and locate a pulse. "Breathe," the rescuer hisses in Clarissa's ear, "breathe, you silver beauty, *breathe*." He slaps both cheeks, pushes against her abdomen, the sternum, and Clarissa shudders, coughing weakly. Leveraging under her arm, the rescuer rolls Clarissa face up and with a sidestroke tows her beside him. Clearly this fellow is a savvy swimmer, outsmarting the current by going out to sea with it, at an oblique angle, until the suction dissipates in deeper water. When well separated from the riptide current he reverses direction, back to shore.

Along the return he encourages her, speaking against her temple, quietly, soothingly. "Relax, shoulders down, let me do the work. Enjoy the trip, lay yourself back, like on a bed, relax, relax. Perfect. That's perfect. See, you're perfect. You do, real deal, look perfect." The rescuer has a sense of humor. Between strokes he teases, "Okay, does saving your life . . . prove . . . I deserve . . . a date with you . . . next week?"

Just beyond the surf line the young man stops, presumably

to adjust his grip on Clarissa before breaking through the waves. Treading water, he lifts Clarissa high upright like a surfacing mermaid, looking all the more so because in her struggles the bikini top had been pushed down to her waist. He rearranges the top to its proper, modest position over her breasts. Her eyes blink. With seawater and his fingertips the rescuer washes her cheeks clean of mucous trails. He tucks errant twists of hair off her face, impractical as that may be, given the waves directly ahead.

On the beach has assembled a crowd of the concerned and the curious, craning their necks, anxious over this delay. A boy at the front, dropping his skimboard and pogoing higher and higher to gain line-of-sight, asks, "Hey, what's that. What, is he kissing her, or what?" A man behind the boy answers, "It's CPR." A woman beside the man asks, "But Brian, CPR on your feet, or I mean, straight up. Will it work?"

At last, here comes the rescuer, into shallow water, carrying Clarissa until he has to give her up into other hands.

"Clarissa. Clarissa. Clarissa?" pleads her mother.

Her whimper indicates that Clarissa is back among the living. The group greets this signal with an instant cheer. They swaddle her in towels, dry her hair with alternate bouts of restraint and rough enthusiasm, their giddy chatter rising in decibels to match their relief. If Mr. Kreshmeyer's sons could see him, their mouths would gape open at their soggy father dashing about, flapping like a whirling dervish as he jumped and whooped, shoving bills at the heroes, enough money to reimburse dozens of cans of beer. "Spend these before they dry out into nothing. Haven't you heard about the shrinking value of the dollar?" Mrs. Kreshmeyer is behaving scarcely better, pushing food at people by the plateful whether or not they might want it—luckily, they do want. "Take, take. Try this pizza. Put whipped cream on these brownies!"

In the distance can be heard, theatrically, an approaching siren. "Too late, you missed the party!" and "Too late, you missed the custard!" and "You missed the horseradish on the brownies!" voices shout, with a combined symphonic hoot for a finale, before they disassemble to other parts of the beach, the excitement thankfully over.

The rescuer himself lingers, reluctant to leave his masterful creation of life. "Her name's Clarissa?" he asks the mother.

Mrs. Kreshmeyer has already given him a flurry of ferocious hugs, until her clothes are nearly as sodden as her husband's. "It's Clarissa Kreshmeyer."

Richard has Clarissa's comb in a pocket. He considers using it to free those knotted swirls in her hair, loosening the strands and like a caress smoothing them out across the flat of his hand. But he keeps the comb where it is.

Too drained to speak, Clarissa had made an attempt with Richard, evidently to communicate something urgent. Only the word "Richie . . ." came out, leaving on her lips a tiny bluish bubble—the hue of skimmed milk—and leaving in her eyes a message that likely meant, "We'll forget this horrible day, both of us."

Everyone Richard ever loved called him by a child's name. After journeying to the continent's other edge he was Richie or a Small Richard again, or always was, and Richard knows better than most that there are days no one forgets, no one, regardless. Of course he should stand up, take out Clarissa's comb. Go to her. Absolutely. Absolutely he should spend many more days with his own parents, be part of their home once again. The "home" is not the house of Richard's childhood, that substantial colonial with its treacherous half-acre of green lawn, but instead the rental apartment his parents could afford after the early retirement, or to use another set of suspect quotation marks—"early retirement." Richard should sit at the dining table while his father mixes a second scotch-and-soda, his mother having already retired to the bedroom after dinner, all according to custom. Absolutely Richard should full out explain why he gave up his basketball scholarship, tell how he began loathing the blood battle of competition. His father will be nodding, sipping, sipping. Soon his father's focus will shift to a point over Richard's shoulder, off in indeterminate space, an escape place where it always settled. And should Richard, also as always before, resent his father's escape? No. He should say, "Forget about basketball. What I want to tell you is, I like it when you get daydreamy tipsy with your Never-Never-Land smile. It reminds me of me. In fact, I like everything about you, the whole package." Next he should, absolutely, march over to his mother's bedroom door, shove it open, lean in, and declare in a shout, "Mother!

Wake up! Listen, anybody who ever thought you stopped being our pretty Helena Holland made a big, big mistake." Richard could do that, and should.

Mrs. Kreshmeyer is inviting Clarissa's rescuer to a celebratory family dinner, writing down her home address and personal phone number. Already she has an elaborate menu in mind and wishes to confirm each dish with the young man's particular tastes. "And I want you and Clarissa to meet properly. That's only right. You'll like each other, I know."

"Generous of you," he says. "I wonder, butting into a family meal. Might make for funny feelings?"

"You *are* a family member, after today, believe you me."

"I heard that the tall guy over there is Clarissa's boyfriend."

Mrs. Kreshmeyer thoughtfully taps her chin with a dance of fingertips. "They're friends, yes."

"I heard, I thought, fiancé."

"No, no."

"No?"

Mrs. Kreshmeyer winks, shyly, or slyly: perhaps for the first time in her adult life such a peculiar wink. "Not strictly. And you *will* come to dinner. I love cooking for special people."

"Then I accept. I'd be a fool to miss your cooking, and anyway I see that you're a woman who gets her way." The young man must be a gentleman, as well as a hero, because he courteously and carefully imitates Mrs. Kreshmeyer's rather bizarre winking display.

Off in his momentary isolation, Richard is startled to have Mr. Kreshmeyer join him, sitting alongside and calling him *Richie*, putting a firm palm on Richard's raised knee. "Richie," says Mr. Kreshmeyer, "I think I understand how you feel right now. Damn it, I do. But don't worry yourself sick about today. Now just head on over there and give Clarissa a—whatever—a hug or some such."

"I want to comb her hair."

"Good, good. I'll make a prediction here, Richie. Give it a chance, a little chance, and today won't amount to anything important. Not in the end."

Mr. Kreshmeyer is correct at least with one prophesy. They did litter those beer cans.

Choosing a Husband Troubles

My mother really does use the words "biological clock," usually accompanied by a significant lift of her eyebrows. "Cindy," she reminds me, "every unmarried woman of *sense* keeps tabs on her biological clock." Sharp arch of eyebrows. On the morning of my 30th birthday last year she popped out with a halfway joke, saying, "Forget about regular biological clocks, because doggone soon you'll be using a kitchen three-minute egg timer. Egg timer, get it?" And just lately, after dinner while we sat in our lounge room, in front of the stone fireplace, sampling those free beers we get from Norm, Momma lowered her voice—although we two live alone—and like revealing the history of a major disease, informs me, "You know, Cindy, and I don't believe you do, my menopause started when I was thirty-nine." That might be correct. But I recall borrowing tampons from her bathroom cabinet even after her last husband Royce got killed.

Heck, I agree with her. Nobody understands more than me that I'm an only child and Momma's one chance at grandkids. And both of us are experts when it comes to the requirements of the breeding process. Here in eastern Oregon we own 800 acres of wide open space where we run 700 head of feeder calves, fattening them up for the beef market. But our real specialty, or anyhow our real reputation, comes from the six prize pedigree bulls we keep to sell their sperm.

Heaven knows I never avoided the boys and they never avoided me. Even as a teenage girl I "stood out," to repeat what I guess was a clever compliment about my figure from a young male classmate. Or as Momma once said, "Cindy, you upped the cup size in the family name"—my name being Cynthia Cuppalow. Along with that I was born with a showy pile of "Dairy Freeze vanilla" curls, quoting here the words of another young pimply guy, and the pile hasn't darkened or melted much over the years. For whatever it's worth, I now have three boyfriends. Yep, at the same time. Momma says that when news got out how I was ready for marrying, I was like a cow in estrus, waiting in the semen collection stall, while the poor dumb bulls stamped around outside bellowing to be let in. That's how talk on a cattle ranch goes sometimes.

And I had an original boyfriend a fair while ago, called "Peetie." Peetie was his little-boy name, but he refused switching to "Peter" when he grew big, and maybe due to the "Peetie" he needed to show how he was a true man. You better believe he was a true man, and we were in it together for the long haul. I mean the long, long haul. Before any marriage Peetie wanted to join the military and prove he could become a U.S. Ranger, parachuting from airplanes, dangerous this and dangerous that, the complete soldier enchilada. He succeeded wonderfully, of course, and received an early promotion. As a reward the government sent him off overseas to a very important war.

People ask how come Momma ended up owning such a great-going cow spread. Well, besides being a smart cookie herself, she had two husbands, my father Bart and my father Royce. No, not both at once. Bart, the first husband, was my actual father, and he bought the land and set up the operation. Less than a week before my 11th birthday he was caught in one of those bad muck-ups that happen left and right on these ranches. His own Dodge four-wheeler rolled over his chest when he crawled under to yank out tumbleweeds stuck on the axle. According to a neighbor driving past, Bart's last words to the world were "those sonsofbitches." Cussing out the tumbleweeds.

My father, as I remember him, was a thoughtful man who stepped around any emotional carryings-on, and I may have inherited a chunk of that from him. Before the Dodge killed my father he had already bought my birthday present, which supports my claim about his being thoughtful. The present was a guitar, which I couldn't play yet, but father Bart had hopes. While he never sang or whistled, now and then he would bend song lyrics in Momma's direction. A for-instance is the Johnny

Cash flood tune that says "How high's the water, Momma?" ("It's 2 feet high 'n' risin'.") So father Bart sings/talks his version with "How high's Momma, Mr. Waters?" ("She's 5' 3" 'n' thrivin'.") In those days Mr. Waters was the preacher at the Resurrected Spirit Reform Church, down the road seven miles. Eventually Mr. Waters moved back to Oklahoma. "Notice how religion has dried up around here of late?" had been father Bart's comment on the matter. He never chuckled, or had any twinkle in his eye, when he said such stuff, and I used to wonder whether I was supposed to laugh, so I didn't. Mamma neither. Nowadays when Momma tells about the Johnny Cash song she always smiles.

My second father, Royce, died in the winter of my senior year of high school. He tipped over our new Case forklift by lifting too heavy a pallet of grain sacks too high up the boom on too uneven a patch of muddy ground. Like I said, these ranches are places where accidents go around just begging to happen. It was the forklift that crushed him, not the pallet. That forklift came through without a scratch and we use the thing still today.

Nobody was flabbergasted when father Royce had his accident, although his departure did create a mountain of inconvenience, including the result that after high school I jumped directly into the family cattle business. Royce had been raised a city boy—if we count Bend, Oregon, as a city—and he worked as a tax adviser before my mother came across him one tricky tax season. He was a sweet fellow who never did brown up and tan right (kept getting sunburns) and who never could change a spark plug without skinning his knuckles. Royce put us on the depreciation highway to income tax paradise and, patient as a saint, he made us computer savvy, but he never took to cows. He tried his best not to gripe about the smell of manure. Momma and I ended up liking him a lot.

"My luck with men has been plain crummy," Momma told me. "Let's hope you do better, eh?"

* * * *

Of my three boyfriends, Norbert is the one I know best, since he's been our vet for almost ten years. "Norb" as we all call him is five years older than I am and due to his successful veterinary practice is the only one of my suitors not short of money in comparison to me. For that reason Norb is Momma's favorite. Plus (according to Momma) "Can you imagine how handy that would be, having a vet living in your own home. Can you? Wow." Plus "Norb's a grownup this minute already with both feet solid on the ground." Plus "Tell me, does that man know how to dress or not. Wow." Plus "Take a look at Norb's eyes. Those are bedroom eyes. Gentle eyes but gentle bedroom eyes. That man learnt about female parts and not just from a cow."

"Maybe you ought to marry him, Momma," I told her. "Wow."

But, as usual, she hit the nail on the head. There *is* a bunch to like, and love, about Norb, and I have no problem nuzzling up under his clean-shaven chin and sniffing that Norwegian Pines cologne he wears. I tuck in tight there with his arm around me and I want him to strum me like I'm that guitar father Bart gave me and that never ever got played.

Four years back Norb's wife killed herself by taking the wrong pain pills. The coroner ruled that Yvonne mixed up her Tylenol tablets with pinkish horse pills from the veterinary supply cabinet, a logical confusion or confused logic triggered somehow by her favorite color being pink. Norb threw himself 200% into his vet practice.

About a year ago Norb began dropping by our place at odd times, without our sending a service request, and I'd catch him politely checking me out in that hunter procedure we girls recognize all about.

"Here we go, Miss Romance," Momma instructed me, enthused.

I checked him out, too, those big brown eyes of his that warm you up like a fuzzy blanket on a January night, those hands that explore tenderly through my curls but are strong enough to pull out a stuck-sideways calf from a birthing mother cow while she kicks like crazy. His voice is low and easy with a soothing sexy sound, and he never mumbles or stumbles with his words and goes exactly to what he intends to say.

"Norb's a man among boys," Momma offered. "I'm betting he's a good kisser."

"He's a darn good kisser."

"Aha."

At least once a week Norb climbs into my pickup truck (a Dodge four-wheeler, same as father Bart's) and we drive out to the back acres, examining the condition of the grass, because our beef operation uses free range feed more than most ranches do. Naturally, being a vet, Norb takes a gander at the young cattle, giving me an off-the-cuff estimate of their weight gain. Here and there we stop the truck, get out, walk around for a nearer look at the livestock, find a high spot to search over the bare countryside that rolls on forever and a mile in this section of Oregon. The sky will be bent down everywhere over the emptiness and the wind usually is tapping on our faces. Norb places his arm around me and we turn our backs to the wind. Then we do some of that kissing.

When Norb stays late—likely invited by Momma for a dinner—we stroll out and snuggle into the swinging loveseat on the veranda, with a nice comfortable view, and sometimes smell, of the nearby loading pens. It was on this loveseat one night, rocking with our boots off, that Norb spoke his mind about the two of us.

"You know what people call this piece of furniture we're sitting on, don't you?" he said, almost too whispery to hear.

Cindy, I told myself, this has the signs of a serious deal going down.

His voice went on in a calm lullaby beside my ear, making me lean into him, and relax, not much different from when a nervous heifer settles down in a squeeze chute. "And people are gossiping that Norbert the vet has fallen for the Cuppalow gal. Even sits in a loveseat with her. And the people are right, Norbert has fallen for the beautiful Cuppolow girl. He wants to take care of her in heart and mind for the rest of their lives."

The sun had sunk beyond the faraway horizon as we sat on the swing, and me, a dumb bunny fumbling around for a proper sentence, fumble up instead one of his hands to hold. Since a single hand didn't add up, it seemed, to the importance of the moment, I located his other hand to hold as well.

Now with the dark closing in, listening to Norb's voice was practically the only part of us left to notice, that and our hands touching. Norb detailed what was "obvious" to everybody about the Norbert and Cindy "team." "Folks can, easily enough, figure out the amazing fit—our businesses, our even-keel temperaments, our man-woman respect for each other, our *everything* together."

There was a little more silence and a little more darkness before Norb wrapped me into his arms. "What the gossipers can never understand is that we have something in common more important than any cow business. Much more important. It deepens us. And it will always bind us close. I had Vonnie and you had Peetie."

I was listening, there in the night, to every steady soft syllable of Norb's, and I heard a bitty crack in the middle of two of those syllables. But the wobble happened so fast, went by so fast, I can't be sure whether it cracked in the middle of Von-nie or Peet-ie.

* * * *

The sort of comical fact about boyfriend #2 is that his name mixes up super easy with boyfriend #1. Already there on the tip of my tongue sits Mr. Norbert/Norb, when along comes Mr. Norman/Norm. What's a girl to do. Be careful. Be careful is what she should do. When a man is nuzzling your earlobe it simply isn't fair to him to get careless with names.

Norb/Norm sound alike, but different they are, these two men, for certain. Norm runs a smallish beer distributorship that his dad passed along to him, last August, when Norm turned twenty-six. I met him at a livestock auction where I was bidding on calves and he was servicing the beer concessionaire. Or I should clarify that Norm met *me*, since a leap-ahead action was Norm's behavior from the start, when he saw me step out of the Dodge truck. On that first afternoon when he charged up to introduce himself he bowled me over, and still now he bowls me over, sometimes nearly does knock me over, "So I can catch you and save you in my arms," he says, with a sunshine smile that makes me tipsier than that free beer he delivers to our house.

"Cindy," he announced on that auction day, "they told me your name, those folks behind me there, and I asked about your name 'cause I'm not a fool, and only a fool would let you walk by without introducing himself. Are you engaged yet to any lucky man? Gosh, thank the Lord for that. You know what? I believe, looking at you here, in front of me, I really should thank the Lord for that."

Here's what shocked me. I told myself, This pretty-boy yokel is a pure Don Juan jackass. But no. It turned out, Norm was clueless about being the handsomest dog east of the Willamette Valley, and his syrupy praise was reserved for Cindy Cuppalow. He did already have a girlfriend all right, Maisy Stubbenfelder, the current Miss Deschutes County beauty queen. A week after our meeting at the auction, when he first drove out to the ranch house with our beer, he carefully informed Momma that Maisy was "the nicest girl," and that he had "let her down easy."

"And with a case of free beer?" Momma had wondered aloud—not to Norm, later to me.

As Norm and I began spending hours together, Momma asked, "Whatever do you see in that boy?" She provided her own answers before I could give any. "Sure, he's a handsome devil, handsomer than those movie stars Hollywood offers up lately. Sure, he's built like Ol' Red up there over the fireplace." Old Red was our original and best-ever champion breeding bull, a rusty-colored giant critter that rescued the ranch's financial skin and put us on solid ground. To honor Old Red and, I suppose, to remind us all to keep focus on our investment strategy, father Bart spent $3000 at a taxidermy shop to mount Old Red's head for the house.

"Momma," I scolded her, "you can't fool me. You've a weak spot for Norm yourself. He turns you straight into a teenage girl, and I see you fixing your hair and your makeup whenever he comes to visit us."

"I didn't claim that I don't like him. Who wouldn't. He's as delicious as a bowl of my favorite Banana Slurp ice cream. With a cherry on top. Two cherries. But, mercy, how much ice cream can a person keep eating, day and night?"

"Listen, Norm bubbles over with loving me. He bubbles. I never had anybody love me so much before. And I'm not talking about dessert love."

In my pickup truck I gave Norm his own tours of the ranch acreage, showing him the ins and outs of the cattle game. Right off I could tell he would need considerable learning to grab ahold of new skills, same as father Royce had needed. Still, Norm is no male-model airhead and he was plenty interested, and asked plenty of sensible questions. On one of our tours I asked Norm if he wanted to see how we collect specimens for our sperm business. I figured, might as well show him the whole caboodle, not put off any of it.

He said, "Shucks, why not."

I said, "Blunt stuff happens, is all."

He said, "Why not."

So we waited in what our bull handler, Renaldo, has titled "the Porno Theater," a separate stall area where a sturdy teaser steer stands tethered, munching alfalfa from a hay rack. A helper leads the stud bull in by a rope, all 2000 pounds of it already stomping around in a hurry because it knows the routine. The helper pulls the bull back from three of its attempts to mount.

"That makes the bull extra randy," I explain to Norm.

"Now it doesn't care whether that's a cow in front or a steer or another bull."

With snorts and grunts the stud bull rises up again, its hooves splaying every-which-way, and Renaldo crouches down with the collection tube ready in his hand.

I tell Norm, "Renaldo wears steel-toed boots but still got his foot broken twice and his collarbone once."

The bull is slinging saliva from its foamy mouth and its forelegs are pawing at the steer and its eyes are rolling wild, when Renaldo darts under with the tube, and back out again. Three seconds, tops. Then the bull is gone and outside again before you can clear your throat. Norm did clear his throat, or he tried to.

"There'll be up to five billion healthy sperm in that rubber sock," I told him afterward. "That's our guarantee to the lab where we sell the tube contents."

On the September afternoon that Norm stopped by with another dozen bottles of beer, Momma was off in town shopping, and he toted the bottles into the pantry and stacked them with the other fifty beer bottles already there.

"Thanks, Norm," I said, giving him a playful push. "That'll last us for the next decade or three."

He grabbed my push hand and kept it. "Sorry, but I'm not giving up my best excuse to come here and be with you." His face was stern.

"Where's your famous smile?" I asked him. "Where're those famous teeth of yours?" Really I knew where the smile was, or why it wasn't. I knew he had reached that certain spot.

"Cindy, I don't want to need excuses for coming here anymore, not anymore, no, no, no. It hurts way too much to be away from you, Cindy." He yanked me into him and tightened me up with such a powerful squeeze that black pinpoints started prancing before my eyes. "Cindy, Cindy," he said, "just let me live with you forever. I make a promise that nobody, not even your momma, will love you more than I love you. I promise." Despite those black spots it was clear for me to see that Norm was teary.

* * * *

Besides rangeland grass for the cattle we irrigate seventy acres of permanent pasture, and buy winter grain to fatten and finish off the herd before it sells to market. The gorgeous, glittering blue Peterbilt 18-wheeler trucking in our grain sacks is how I connected with suitor #3.

When Momma saw me meeting up with the driver she cocked her head like a hungry robin listening for a worm underground. "*Three* men in your corral?" she guessed. "Is that what this is. True, I went through *two* husbands, so you're planning ahead?" She asked about his name and I wiggled around, not answering right away, which made her suspicious.

"You hiding something bad from me?" Momma asked. "Come out with it, come on."

"It's not bad."

"Then tell me."

"You'll fling back a silly comment."

"I certainly will not."

"His name's Peter."

"Good grief. Peter again. Peter and a Peterbilt. Dear, dear. The silly comment you don't want me to make is about you acting silly?"

What I didn't let leak to Momma was that this Peter had done two tours of Army duty in Afghanistan, although she found out the facts eventually. And if Momma was right as usual, or half-right as usual, and I was a silly girl, at least label me a happy silly girl, because I did get pleasure using that name once more.

And yes, I shoehorned "Peetie" into Peter, even if he squawked quite a bit before giving in, complaining that "Peetie" sounded like a kid with training wheels still on his bike. He asked, "What's wrong with my regular name Peter?"

"I like using Peetie."

"Don't be embarrassed. I learned to ignore peter jokes way back by age eight. Still these days some knucklehead, pointing at my truck, will shout 'Who built your peter, Peter?' A knucklehead can't help himself."

"I just like using Peetie."

"Can we compromise by using Pete. Not a favorite shorthand of mine, but a classic."

"Peetie is cuter."

"Cuter. All right, if cute is what Cindy wants, Cindy gets cute. *Some*body must find himself wanting to spoil cute Cindy to let her have her cute way. Who knows, possibly this *some*body can convert her back to saying Peter at a future date."

When I drove Peetie along the old routes over the ranch, he had a habit of stopping the Dodge to hike, off in the middle of nowhere, forcing me to scuffle along behind him with dirty boots. I could find no real sense to it because the Dodge would have brought us to the same spot anyway, no problem, and now the pickup was far back out of sight laughing at us.

"Peetie," I said, "my Dodge would've driven here easy."

He grunted his agreement.

"Peetie," I said, "why this walking urge?"

"I enjoy walking. But it's not an urge. My list of urges adds up on the brief side."

"Peetie, maybe you liked marching in the Army."

"I doubt that."

"Peetie, did you walk much in Afghanistan?" Obviously I made myself a first-class pest with the constant Peetie-Peetie-Peetie. I could hear myself being a pest. But I could never resist forming that sound again with my own lips and tongue.

"The Infantry always walks. Walks and walks."

"Peetie, tell me some things about Afghanistan, about how it was over there, away from here, or how strange maybe from where we sit, right on this ranch."

"Another time."

"Peetie, I just want a little picture of the place, just a little piece of a little day over there."

"Another time."

I waited for that other time to come. On a later trip, while sitting together on a flat rock in one of those nowhere spots with the Dodge out of view, Peetie did reveal he had been a captain in the Army before dropping from the career path. I told him, "My goodness, I should salute whenever we meet."

"My Captain Days are long behind me."

"You captain your Peterbilt now."

"I'll put that behind me, too. I have other plans."

When I asked about the plans, Peetie said he was "planning the plans still," but they included "using my brains more than sitting on my ass in a truck" and "finding that woman I can't live without." I figured this was the logical cue Peetie had set up for himself to declare Cindy as "that woman." First he waved his hand around us, indicating my 800 acres. He asked, or wondered out loud, "You ever get lonely here?"

Now comes the proposal, I predicted. To help shove the script forward, I said, "A person feels lonely only when a person is alone, regardless of the whereabouts, right?"

I sat on the rock, waiting for Peetie to turn, turn to me, up close, do a kiss or a clench. He stayed staring out over the 800 acres. His eyes are about the color of his Peterbilt tractor cab, a big difference from my real Peetie's honey-hazel eyes with their endless lashes that every girl envied, but regardless a nice Peterbilt blue. It was a sunny sky above us, sitting on the rock, and I had stuck a spare cowboy hat on Peetie's head, and from under the hat tumbled messy waves of his sandy sort-of-blonde hair that he forgets to have cut. A handsome fellow, all in all, with shoulders too broad for me to stretch an arm straight across, is how I describe him—nearly as handsome as my real Peetie, while of course not as handsome as Norm.

Never turning to me, Peetie ruined our script by saying, "Me, I like the loneliness of this landscape, or anyhow the bareness of it, or the empty feel around us in every direction."

To complete the usual full inspection of our cattle business I took Peetie to the Porno Theater. The show this time was put on by a different bull with the same patient steer and with the same slobbery pawing. At the conclusion Peetie said, with a chuckle, "Not much of a thrill found here for anyone, is there. Possibly for Renaldo?"

I had practically given up waiting for Peetie's proposal moment, when a month or so after the Porno Theater event he sprung it on me in broad daylight. And it *was* broad daylight, noon, as we walked across the loading area toward his parked rig. Suddenly he stopped short, squinting down at me in the sun because my extra cowboy hat for him was left back in the Dodge. He wagged a friendly finger at me, announcing, "I bet you'll never guess how I discovered that I love you."

This statement was news of all kinds to me, and beyond my guessing, let alone answering.

"Because," he said, "because every day I can't wait for you to call me *Peetie*. This is no joke. Hearing that *Peetie* means I belong to *you*. And I *want* to belong to you. What's in a screwy name? Everything, it turns out. Go figure. Now what? I need to find out if you love me back, and at the moment your face is out of focus in this damn glare."

* * * *

Momma and I began splitting just one of Norm's beers, instead of drinking a whole bottle each, because the bathroom scale was creeping in the wrong direction. Momma sipped, leaned backward on the couch, set her socked feet up on a rawhide upholstered stool, relaxed, took a breath, readied herself to enjoy the weekly report on what man was "leading the pack at the finish line."

"You are at the finish line, I imagine," she prodded.

"I am?"

"You aren't. Hm. Look at what girl went and put herself in a pickle."

"Into an entire pickle barrel."

Mamma sipped, and sipped. She started examining Old Red up on the wall almost like she had never noticed that massive bull's head before. Funny thing is, Momma had constantly grumbled after father Bart mounted Old Red above the fireplace, swore about "those glarin' glass eyes following your backside wherever you walk in the room, giving a woman the creepies." Later when father Royce offered to move Old Red to the barn, "where he fit in better," Momma said, "No, let him stay here."

From thinking about Old Red up there, I reckon, Momma turned and asked me, "So which gentleman provides the best breeding bump?"

What a question from your own mother.

Momma pulled her feet off of the rawhide stool. "No answer. You don't know yet. Say, Miss Cindy, think back on that expensive bull we bought from the Circle K. Think back. He showed perfect, didn't he, had monster weight, was hung right. Then he backs away. We even tied up a cow fresh in heat and he still backs away, like he sniffed poison."

"We got our money back from Circle K."

"Cindy, sweetie, you don't get your money back when your husband doesn't do his doodle business proper."

"Actually, Momma, I think you can get your money back. D-i-v-o-r-c-e."

"Ha-ha. This is no game, Cindy. Ask me, I could tell you a story or two."

"Oh, have mercy. I'm *not* asking. Don't tell me your doodle stories. Please do not."

But could Momma be half-right again?

Each of them—Norb, Norm, Peetie—had given me critical defensive space during our kissing and squeezes, with no moves below my waist and no wandering fingers on my cuppalows. Granted, I had never flashed any of those go-ahead signals that a woman can switch on, such as a nip on an ear rim or an out-of-control suck on a tongue, or that absolute winner, letting a hand accidentally slide from the top ridge of a thigh and head down, inside, in the direction of his crotch. With my first Peetie those green traffic lights went blinking on at the same time, plus a few others.

Getting the prescription for birth control pills made me skittish, after x-number of years without one, figuring I had provided whisper fuel for Dr. Fennell and his gabby office staff. However, I had no intention of prowling around with a pocketful of condoms, obviously armed for a seduction attack.

* * * *

Norb has a wonderful home, fussed over by a daily cleaning maid, the house surrounded by flawless gardens, maintained by a professional yard crew.

"I'm confessing to this expensive help," he tells me, "so you won't think I have the skills to do such orderliness myself. And normally I eat dinner in town. Since Vonnie died. But tonight I invited you here and did my amateur darnedest to prepare a meal of scampi pasta with Parmesan and garlic cloves and a sixty-dollar bottle of white wine, a foolhardy cooking gamble for me, sure, yet a way to prove what a special guest you are." As an exclamation point he kisses me on the temple. In appreciation I plant a wet kiss on his neck.

On our steps to the dining table he returns a lingering kiss on my own neck. The meal, bless dear Norb, has its shortcomings. Scampi is a tough dish to hit on the mark without turning rubbery, I realize. And I swallow a chunk of garlic clove that has my eyes watering for the remainder of the meal. Of course I praise Norb's cooking talents to the high heavens. He looks skeptical. The wine is worth the sixty bucks and for that reason, among others, we empty the bottle in a bit of a rush.

After a dessert cup of lemon sherbet our conversation begins to hit gaps, which is not typical of Norb, and I jump into a gap, saying, "In case you intend to kiss me again tonight, then I need to brush my teeth with a strong toothpaste. Or did you cook with garlic to prevent any kissing?"

Norb laughs and laughs. "I warned you that I was a fool amateur in the kitchen. And I do have plenty of toothpaste because I do intend."

The toothpaste, Norb goes on, "is in the *en suite* bathroom" of his bedroom, where a second toothbrush already waits in the holder. "Okay to use that one?" I ask. Reaching my arm around for the toothbrush my breasts have to squish up against his back. Or they "have to" squish if I avoid the bother of shifting sideways.

We both laugh now at the sight of us in the mirror, toothpaste bubbles on the lips, the sight of us spitting in the sink together, the sight of us rinsing our mouths with water from the same glass, spitting again.

I say, "I've never done this with a man before, spitting together. Very intimate."

Norb says, "Very erotic."

Zip, we're on his bed, clothes being peeled off. At the last instant before the last pieces of underwear disappear, we both decide, with one voice, "Let's kill the lights."

In the blackness we listen to each other's sounds. A gasp from him. A gasp from me. A moan from him. A moan from me. But I soon find out what a mistake it was turning out the lights. Because the moan I hear isn't Norb's. The face I imagine on the bed with me, over me, isn't Norb's face. I feel like a horrible cheat to Norb, except I can't send the other face away, not in this empty dark. And I'm having a second horrible feeling, about whether Norb breathing hard over there next to me is also seeing another face, not mine. Now . . . I'm identifying the handle color of that barely used toothbrush from the bathroom, the toothbrush I just had in my mouth. Pink. Pure pink.

* * * *

"Should I dim these lights?" asks Norm in his bedroom, as courteous, careful, nice-boy cautious as he has been for every minute of the evening.

"No, no," I say, "leave all the lights on."

For his birthday Norm had taken me to dinner at the most expensive restaurant within a 100-mile radius. "I should be treating *you* to dinner for a birthday present," I had protested, and meant it. He said, "Not on your life." Standing by my chair he seated me with a guiding arm on my shoulder, and I reached around his waist to give a thank-you hug when my hand slipped down and I more or less had to grip his muscular left butt cheek. We ordered sirloin steak because Norm thought I would appreciate "supporting the beef market." Across the table, during the whole meal, his eyes had been on me and hardly on his pricey steak, which he never did finish eating. "Don't worry," he had said, "I won't interrupt dinner by repeating and repeating how much I love you and how I want to marry you." We sampled some red wine. "We deliver beer to this place," Norm had explained, as information. Then, "But what I truly want to say is, how happy it makes me to watch you across the table. Even watching you chew makes me warm and happy. I won't keep interrupting you by repeating how happy I am. I am though."

After our meal Norm had politely helped me into my evening coat and for an amusing gesture I helped Norm into his, straightening out where the coat had bunched at the beltline. Muscular right butt cheek.

"Ready for that dancing?" Norm had asked.

"Or let's tour the fancy condo of yours that you brag about."

"Really?"

"Really."

At his condo Norm had shown me his stainless steel kitchen appliances, apologizing for a stack of dirty dishes in the sink, had pointed out in the living room the details of a purple-and-orange color scheme, which I blame Miss Deschutes County for once supervising, and he had led me to the large picture window with its second-floor overlook of town lights. There he had stood behind me, kissing the nape of my neck.

"Don't you include the bedroom as part of your tour?" I had asked, while demurely facing away, in the direction of the town.

"Really? You mean, really?"

At the bedroom doorway Norm must have been inspired,

because he picked me up Tarzan-style, or he had in mind bride-across-the-threshold style, carrying me inside and depositing me gingerly as a carton of eggs on the bed.

"Should I dim the lights?" he asks, thoughtful of my modesty.

"No, no," I say, "leave all the lights on."

Which he is happy to do. Yet he hesitates, waiting for another green light or two from me. My green light ideas have run out so I pull his fingers down to my buttons and snaps.

At first Norm undresses me as fussily and slowly as he would his sister's doll, if he had a sister, folding my clothes into a neat stack on a dresser top. Next he starts kissing me on the lips before gradually moving on to kiss me in every location imaginable. He applies all his skills and he does have skills to apply. Norm works himself into a—well, into a worker's sweat, and I admit, I didn't mind the sweat, it having a genuine ranch flavor and done for my benefit. Clearly, Norm here is doing his mightiest not to make a wrong move by behaving no better than the bull he saw paw and snort in the Porno Theater. Although for all eyes to see, naked Norm was born a bull, in the best sense, and Norm finally performs tonight exactly as proud Old Red always did with his assignment.

Norm begins immediately with his doubts and responsibilities. "Sorry if I didn't do my half of the dance right," he says. Since I never had the talent or the heart to manage skillful fakery in bed, Norm has his suspicions.

I scoff at his worries. Fake scoffing I handle reasonably well, and Norm is a sweetie pie who deserves an appreciative woman.

"I'd hate," he says, "to enjoy anything more than you enjoy it, Cindy. That'd hurt me."

Extra intense scoffing comes from Cindy. The sweetness of this sweetie pie is causing my own hurting.

Norm lies on the bed, on his back, quiet, seeming to arrange his thoughts, and says at last, "My daddy told me about your soldier boyfriend. When Daddy saw us two going together, he told me. I want to swear to you, Cindy, that I love you so much you can keep loving him, for as long as you need to, however long, if you have love left to love me alongside. I'm not jealous. We won't have to turn our backs on a hero."

* * * *

I intend to bring the total exhausting husband hunt to a quick conclusion. My patience is shot, my emotions wrung dry, and I don't sleep worth crap anymore what with the tossing and turning. I arrange for Peetie to meet me at the ranch. Into the Dodge pickup I load two pillows, three fluffy blankets, a box of Kleenex tissues, and a roll of peppermint breath mints. Off we go.

I make certain we park at the most isolated of those nowhere places on my 800 acres. Peetie tries to wander away, as is typical, but I grab him back and insist we sit by the Dodge, "for once."

Peetie remarks, "Well, now, can I point out that you're

acting peculiar?"

I think: You ain't seen nothin' yet, Buster.

We sit on the blankets and pick up with our usual distance gazing. But remember, my patience is shot. I consider my green light options and conclude that the choices are limited in the middle of an eastern Oregon high plateau, and furthermore the hell with green lights. "I want to catch some sun," I say, shucking off my red flannel shirt.

"Kind of cool for that?" wonders a curious Peetie.

It is too cool. My red bra follows my red flannel shirt.

Now Peetie is very curious. "Did I already mention you were acting peculiar?"

"Join me. Act peculiar with me."

"Brrr, Cindy, this isn't beach weather."

"Should I put my shirt back on?"

Peetie shakes his head, a definite negative.

"You said you loved me, Peetie."

"I do love you, you little wanton woman. Or you little wanton woman with not-little breasts. If we both strip off our tops, you know what happens next, darling. Is that what you planned out here with this pile of blankets and pillows?"

I nod my head, a definite positive.

His naked chest and my naked chest and the cold air connect and combine with quite a tingle. I ease his head down on a pillow and roll over him, repeating, "Peetie—Peetie—Peetie." Between each repetition of his name, we kiss, hard and harder. "Peetie, Peetie, Peetie." Then I kiss his stubbled cheek, his sharp jawbone, down to his soft throat, down to his collarbone. Directly below the collarbone, where my lips are moving now, is a blank white circle the exact size and shape of a 25-cent coin. I kiss it. "What's this circle?"

"A circle."

"Peetie, from what? A circle from what?"

"A scar that healed nice and tight."

I kiss the perfect circle of a scar. "What makes a circle scar?"

"A bullet from my warrior days. In Afghanistan."

I roll back down beside Peetie. I ask him for the particulars and he leans up on an elbow, surprised, saying, "Cindy, right this minute?"

"We can wait a minute."

"You want to stop kissing in order to hear me report about—what. About how a sixty-year-old Taliban sniper with a third of his rotten teeth missing sent a round through my shoulder?"

"Peetie, I want to hear you talk about Afghanistan."

"We hunted the old joker down and chopped him into hamburger with seven M16's and a heavy M240. That's the beginning and the happy end of the story."

"Yes, but Peetie, I want to hear more about *Afghanistan*."

Reaching over with a lone hand he places its thumb under one of my eyes and its forefinger under the other, the downward weight of his hand opening my eyes wider.

"Peetie, can you please tell me how it was there? Talk to me for a few moments."

"It's your pretty eyes that are doing the talking. They tell me . . . you had someone in Afghanistan. A soldier I suppose. Yes? Yes. You have no brothers. Maybe a boyfriend. Yes? Yes." Peetie removes his hand from under my eyes and caresses my cheek, or pats it, with the type of comforting pat you give to a sad child. "And what happened over there to him?" He checks my face again. "Ah. Christ." Stretching out, he retrieves my red bra for me to put back on, a first from any man in my lifetime.

We sit for a while on the blankets, wearing shirts again, even adding our coats as the late afternoon wind kicks up across the flatness, coming from the direction of Idaho.

"Cindy," says Peetie at last, "I already traveled, myself, every inch, up and down, through how you feel. And I traveled beyond that point, to a spot where I can be a bastard. I'm happy your guy never made it back."

"What does that *mean*, Peetie?"

"Don't let me have to lie. I hope you want honesty and not only sympathy. The simple fact is, if your man, who you miss so much I can smell it, weren't buried, he'd be here and not me. His bad luck made my good luck. You can hate me."

"I think I will hate you."

We climb into the Dodge. The rough, jerky, wordless ride back takes what folks sometimes call "an eternity."

* * * *

Momma understands her daughter as mothers should

understand their daughters. We settle into our seats in the evening, in our lounge, under Old Red, drinking Norm's beer. Momma sticks to her half-bottle and I finish its other half plus bottle number two. Momma watches me put empty bottle number two on the rawhide table without using a coaster, and she says, "I won't criticize about making wet rings on Bart's table because I see how upset you are."

I remove the bottle. "Upset, disappointed. Disappointed, tuckered out."

"No love for any of those three men?"

"I need a fourth to try out. That could be the answer. Or a fifth."

"Oh, my."

"I know, Momma. My biological clock."

"Never mind the clocks. Which one of the three loves you the most, or is that a mystery. *Do* they love you?"

"I suppose they do. Peetie hasn't answered any of my messages yet."

I carry the empty bottles into the kitchen, opening the refrigerator door, contemplating a third beer, when Momma shouts out, "I heard the side toilet flush in there, and could that be a sign of enough beer for tonight?"

"You're such a mother, Momma," I shout back.

"I declare."

I return with a fresh third bottle, plop down, tip up the bottle for a two-gulp swallow, followed by a stifled ladylike belch, probably acceptable even at a public gathering.

"Oh, dear," says Momma.

I say, "I have the perfect method to get Peetie to answer back."

"You want him to answer back?"

"I send him another message."

"Okay, honey."

"I send him another message. This message reads, 'Hey, Peter, listen to me.' That's what the message will say."

"Go on."

"No more going on."

"What? 'Hey, Peter, listen to me.' That's a whole finished-up message?"

"I can make it shorter. I can leave off the 'listen to me' part."

Lonely Scavenger Seeks a Wife

i

It was on a day worthy of pure musical doggerel: singing out "June/afternoon, high/sky." On this rhyming June afternoon, the sun high in a Saturday sky, with heat on his skin, a flow in his blood, he saw her at the corner of 19th and Balboa driving a new flame-yellow Corvette Stingray convertible, a car that cost more than his year's salary. Its personalized license plate read LUV ME. At the stoplight he came up tightly behind her, his restored Firebird Trans Am only a yard short of LUV ME, his eye on her cascade of honeyed hair.

With the switch to a green signal, the Corvette drove slowly, slowly, forcing them both to hit another red light at the next intersection. Without hesitation he pulled alongside for a peek at her face, because this is what he did nowadays in life, sneak looks at the faces of young women. Just last night he lay awake until—when, almost two?—flipping through these stolen images for the right face to dream about, whereupon the two of them could at last drop peacefully asleep in a secure domestic tangle of arms and legs.

Now sometimes girls who drive beautiful cars do so because they themselves decidedly are not. But what dumb luck, the woman in the Corvette revealed herself to be as shimmering as the perfect June day, and yes, he absolutely would luv her, with her flaxen hair fanned out in the sun and those queenly cheekbones that scattered his wits away. Clinching the deal, she turned and smiled at him, fully, brilliantly, freely. She reminded him of that Clairenelle Shampoo commercial, where a knockout blonde, frisky and elated after an invigorating shampoo, waltzes down New York City sidewalks with her clean radiant tresses in a swirl, until bumping into a tall man, smiling at him while he stares back, riveted, and the world realizes that these two will never again be strangers or separated.

The signal changed and he was left flat, gawking, as finally a horn tooted behind him. Once again the Corvette puttered along to miss the next green light. Since he owed the woman a return smile he swung the Firebird beside her. Immediately she looked over to welcome him, and viewing her face a second time, with its sunshine greeting, he forgot to smile back. Off she went.

His Firebird Trans Am—with its heavily modified Cross

Fire V8 engine—wanted to unwind, clear the carbon from its throat, but he held back on the pedal and the Firebird and the Corvette arrived as a pair at another red light. In actual fact the light had not quite turned yellow when they both braked anyhow, their eyes joining. My god, this was a copy of that *Motor Trend* ad he had once read, the one with that flirtatious, romantic scene, photographed at a stoplight, of a distinguished man in an Alfa Romeo 8C Competizione leaning out and conversing with a blonde lady in an apple-red Alfa Romeo Spider convertible.

"Hello . . ." he mouthed across the distance and the feisty engine idle noise of their Corvette and Firebird. "Hello . . ." she mouthed in return. Behind them beeped an impatient Honda hatchback.

At the next intersection he told her, soundlessly, "Hello again," and her lips opened, lingering around the oval shape O: "Hello." He asked, "Your name?" She gave a name that began with B, which happily resembled blowing a kiss. "Yours?" she asked, pointing. "Tim-o-thy," he said. She raised quizzical eyebrows: "Come-to-me?" Away they rolled.

At 24th and Toffler they both laughed, rather like lovers acknowledging a (naughty?) secret.

By 25th and Via Verde she had removed her windbreaker and sat there in a bikini halter with its thin corded straps a scant interruption against nude shoulders, the gold of the sun mixed into her hair. "You're beautiful," he told her, or himself.

At 26th and Capricorn he repeated, calling aloud now,

"You're beautiful," and she answered, "Thank you."

At 27th and San Miguel he said, nodding emphatically, "Yes, beautiful." She sent him a real kiss.

At 28th and Halcyon he dared to shout, "You're a goddess!" She shouted back, "Catch me!"

The Corvette launched ahead in a yellow blur as he hit his own throttle, the Trans Am digging in, lifting its nose, aimed straight at LUV ME. They accelerated so fast that at 29th and Bennington the cars arrived at the start of a red light, and she shot across regardless, taking an instant to turn her head around and trail a seeking arm toward him. He followed all right, the Firebird on the Corvette's rear as the two snaked through traffic, his tires making sideshift squeals, because the Trans Am was heavier, not able to corner as well. She would weave, smoothly, gain space on him, while he would drop down a gear, muffler popping, follow the weave, line up behind the Corvette again, stomp on the gas and catch up.

He had seen this chase before—on a Porsche television commercial. A woman in a purple plum Targa 4S (cabriolet) is being tantalizingly followed by a gentleman wearing a tuxedo and driving a sapphire silver Carrera GTS (turbo), the Porsches whizzing along a curvy country road past gnarled oak trees and pastures with grazing thoroughbreds. The woman tosses her hair, showing to the viewer her arousal from this tease-and-tempt game. Up the ascending road the two cars race on, the camera pulling back to a wider angle, until in the final shot the audience sees a hilltop, the Porsches stopped, parallel, doors open, as outside the woman in an evening gown pirouettes like a ballerina, her hand held by her gentleman.

Recognizing a good story when he has a role in it, he chased the yellow Corvette, the sounds of tires, the gearbox, the eager revved motor, all wailing in sync with his RPM heart rate. Up ahead her blonde hair elevated in the wind, a sensuous banner waving its tactile promises to him. Catlike, she switched lanes. He swung the Firebird after her. Too late he saw the double-parked delivery van, too late to avoid clipping the Firebird's complete right side in a horrific, prolonged screech. He pulled over and ahead the Corvette did the same.

The car's sheet metal looked as if it had been striated by a dozen angry claw hammers, the most painful part being that the Firebird belonged not to him, but to Conrad and Arlene, his younger brother and sister-in-law. Married under two years, they worked staggered shifts at a food services distributor, and never should have broken their budget with this crazy Trans Am hobby. Arlene would, he well knew, get weepy at the sight of this butchered car. Although in general a bundle of unadulterated affirmation, she was fastidious to the core, devotedly vacuuming the household apartment almost every weekday and always on Saturdays and Sundays.

Finding at present nowhere else to turn, he started toward the Corvette, only to see it squat, peel rubber, and leave with its 6.2 liters stoked and ablaze.

"Your car's gonna be somewheres near two months at the

body shop," volunteered a scruffy, cigarillo-sucking, curbside pundit.

ii

Allowing the plausible theory of a chemical connection between diet and mood, he faulted his bachelor menu (the hamburger bought on the run, the frozen omnibus boxes fixed at home) for some of his lethargy and achiness of the heart. Arlene, his loyal sister-in-law, ready with sympathy and a hug, suggested he shop for groceries in the giant Health Food section at the Greenway store.

In September he began doing exactly that, on one visit chancing to stand beside a young woman hardly five feet tall, with loose brunette hair down to her waist and pixie features as clean as a just-scrubbed child. She had a plump lower lip which she nibbled while reading labels.

"I work downtown at the post office," she offered, on her own. "Maybe you noticed me at the counter there."

"Oops, sorry," he said.

"Now and again I get those squinty puzzled stares from folks." She presented him with a no-holds-barred grin, her teeth splendidly uniform, gleaming. Unfortunately, she chose to lick across those white teeth with the tip of a strong fleshy tongue, and he experienced, in a scary surge, a potent impulse to kiss her. Lord almighty, she was a fresh flower, a tiny Earth Mother free of makeup, decorated only by a band of freckles atop the bridge of her button nose.

Bold 'n' Bright toothpaste had a TV spot showing a farmer's daughter (wearing coveralls, a polka-dot kerchief around her neck) who brushes her teeth while smiling vigorously throughout, so vital are her animal energies. The toothbrush whips up and down against her teeth pushing foam over her lips, a picture for some reason not unattractive. When next seen the farmer's daughter is bending out the window of a battered Ford pickup, waving hello to a neighborhood boy, who shyly waves back. The pickup brakes to a near halt. A closeup is focused on her smile and teeth, and like the frisky young colt that she is, she stretches out farther and plants a kiss on the boy's cheek, as his expression changes from stupid surprise to stupid delight.

"My name's Timothy," he said.

"Mine's Nella." Speaking to him, she had to tilt her face far up, throat exposed down to her cleavage, and in the natural act of that short sentence, obliged him by parting her lips again, revealing those teeth and tongue.

"Lovely name," he said.

"Really? Not many tell me that." She was holding a can partly labeled *Curd* and a package with the word *biotin* on it. "Anyways, I'm stuck with Nella, good or bad."

"You're a believer, I'm guessing, in health claims that these natural foods here make some kind of real difference over regular groceries."

"Hey, I surely do believe it. Why put a bunch of weird

chemical preservatives into your protoplasm. For about three years now I've been careful with my food and I've had, like, two wimpy colds in that whole period, nothing else." With an innocuous spread of her arms she presented her petite body, succulent and braless. "I *feel* healthy."

As dumb a donkey as the country bumpkin in the commercial, he said, "You have the healthiest teeth I ever saw."

She took not the least offense, answering, "Thank you. I drink goat's milk, lots of it, plus, of course, other calcium products."

"Of course. And I notice something else about you. But, no, I won't get into it."

"Heck, go ahead. Shoot."

"Well, your skin. It looks cleaner than ordinary clean . . . sort of vibrant. A guy has to catch his breath, seems like." His own breathing was proving the point.

She accepted the compliment without a hint of a blush on her praiseworthy skin. "Plenty of organic fruits, for starters."

There had been a paperback book he picked up at his brother's apartment, a women's romance titled *Wild Freedom* that Arlene left on the kitchen counter, and he spent half a surreptitious Sunday afternoon paging through it. "Great mushy story, yeah?" Arlene had said, while Conrad, his brother, catching sight of the explosively scarlet cover, snickered and snorted. "But it is," had insisted Arlene, with a collaborative wink at Timothy. Little Conrad, who now stood several inches over six feet, had reminded his wife that "Timothy was the older, wiser brother," and that Timothy "sure as crap" never actually read that book.

Admittedly, the single scene in wretched *Wild Freedom* worth remembering is when the romantic couple meet, aboard a night flight from New York to Paris where they happen to be seating companions. The man is a young attorney from Chicago on an overdue vacation. The woman is a kindergarten schoolteacher, a rustic innocent from Whitefish who has been outside of Montana once in her life (a childhood summer trip to Disneyland) and who has no clue about her splendid redheaded impact—probably imagines all women have faces like hers, with oval eyes the color of meadow grass in May, freckles in glorious bloom, a smile as plentiful and spontaneous as noontime sparkles on a river. The attorney "can't help" himself. It tumbles out. He tells her, "I can't help this. I have to tell you. Here I am crossing the Atlantic Ocean to find some grand *haute couture* Parisienne to sweep my heart away, when down beside me on the airplane sits a slip of a lass from Whitefish, Montana, who captures that heart before I land in France. Please forgive my rudeness." She forgives him. He says, "I've never, never, never spoken this way to a woman before, and we hardly know each another. Don't judge me a scoundrel." She does not judge him a scoundrel—sometimes feelings just come a-bustin' out, she concurs. "I want very much to tell you more," he goes on, "but don't dare." She grants permission, even insists. (This *wild freedom* of total honesty between a man and a woman is the big deal in the book.) His voice lowers, to a whisper, forced under by his deeper intensity, not due to the nearby passengers. "I must be loony, confessing these thoughts. Frankly you seem too good to be possible. Are you real?" She answers, "Yes, I'm real." He repeats, "I sound like a loony person. I guess you've bewitched me." She says, "And you're making my heart beat tum-tum-tum, like Blackfoot Indian drums." He asks, "May I dim our cabin lights?" She nods, demurely. He asks, "May I kiss your hand to be certain you genuinely are real?" She nods again, at a loss herself to explain this sudden combustion between them, almost a phenomenon of the airplane's pressurized atmospherics. He asks, "Your lips next? Please?" She does not deny him nor her own emotions and their kiss refuses to separate for the entirety of page 41. Then he raises her hand again to his lips, and reverentially, makes a gentle bite along her delicate knuckles. "I must be *loony*," he repeats. She corrects him, "*L-o-v-e* is the proper spelling maybe." It is, since the schoolmarm and the lawyer, after suitable plot complications in Paris, wed in the happy end.

"Also Vitamin E extracts do super things for skin," further explains Timothy's miniature postal worker, "and taking hot baths. Baths stimulate the surface capillaries."

"They make your skin tingle."

"Right. All tingly."

He could smell the freshness of her, standing beside him, and he said, "My skin feels tingly right now. I think I'm catching it from you—for such a small person you put out awfully big waves. Excuse me for talking this way."

"Oh, that's okay," she said, crouching over to a lower shelf, reaching after a sack of unbleached bran flour. In a pair of junior jeans there was nothing childlike about her from behind.

"You should always wear those jeans. Whoa, what the hell am I saying. My apologies."

Accompanied by her giggle, she rose, her upturned face beneath his, closer than ever, aglow from its downward collection of blood.

"I can't help myself," he announced. Bless it, that was the truth, not the scarlet book. "I'm . . . dizzy. You're making me lose my senses, or my good sense, anyhow."

"Better let me steady you." She took a quite commanding grip on his left elbow.

"Sorry, sorry, but I'm thinking a screwy thought. I'm wondering what freckles taste like when you kiss them."

"Gosh, ask Farley about that," she said, indicating a block of a man approaching them from up the aisle. "He's been my roommate for years, or more a type of husband, I suppose." She introduced the two of them, affably.

"Hi ya," greeted this Farley, a fellow not much taller than his roommate, but who pretty much filled the aisle horizontally.

She informed her type-of-husband, "Timothy's been

learning about health foods."

Soon she might continue, "Timothy here fancies my healthy erotic teeth," and her Farley would say, "Ah-ha-ha. Does Timothy fancy keeping his own teeth?" To avoid having to punch this squat blob, he saluted, politely, and drifted toward the vegetable section, where on occasion the clerks misted the leafy produce and it smelled like a damp melancholy day in spring.

iii

In December, Arlene enrolled him in a singles-only exercise class that met Tuesdays&Fridays in the evenings. Mainly the class members were female, a gender inequity Arlene had counted on, in all likelihood.

He went without enthusiasm, until on the second Tuesday when a late enrollee appeared, a statuesque stunner, and he could only ask himself, "Good grief, what's that woman doing here with a figure like hers?" Inescapably he heard lyrics from the hit song "Sudden Girl":

> *Into the lonely room*
> *she came*
> *(I didn't even know her name)*
> *but before the night was over*
> *we were never again the same.*

She had ebony hair and ebony eyes, creating a dramatic Spanish or Grecian contrast to her creamy complexion, was limber, long-limbed, and wore turquoise leotards, or whatever the term is for those solo outfits that often, bless them, ride up over the globular haunches of curvesome ladies. She could bend at the waist—legs locked together—and place her forehead against her knees.

"You realize, you should be the instructor yourself," he told her. "My name's Timothy."

With hardly a pause in her customary constant motion, she replied, "I do work at keeping fit," removed a sweat band to blot her neck and the bare inner expanse of her fabulous thighs, meanwhile forgetting in those busy actions to provide a name in return.

On Friday he invited her out for a late snack, but she declined, saying "better not put any lost calories back on again." On Tuesday he asked her to hear the children's choir singing Christmas carols at the park. She declined. On Friday, laughing, he offered to escort her to "anyplace in the continental United States," and she, laughing, apologetic over another refusal, complained about being "so very horribly tied up with holiday chores."

In the exercise lines he positioned himself close behind her—visual intoxication—watching her hair bounce, her back and leg muscles ripple, watching her vigorous straight-spine hip rotations with her busty torso first in sharp profile right, then sharp profile left, against a blurry distant gym wall. He began reclaiming her this way, high-kicking and performing her aerobic dance, bosom in independent motion, in his sleep. On a Tuesday, noting her moist face with its creaminess gleaming like a valuable pearl, he proposed going for a cool beer, but she said she drank diet soft drinks, and he realized where he had seen her before, or bodies identical to hers. It was those diet drink ads, Coke or Pepsi or Sprite or whichever, with those leggy girls who had never in their lives needed to diet, frolicking over a beach in their bathing suits where they always jiggle into the arms of waiting boys.

He continued pursuing her because (think about it) why else would she join a singles-only group, except to be pursued. That emboldened him. Furthermore, to misplace modesty for the moment, he was by a mile the most attractive man in this exercise class. Maybe not any major feat in this case, but he did qualify as a decent prospect, more handsome than his brother, for instance, as Arlene, to jack up his sluggish self-confidence, had pointed out.

Although during their class breaks she usually chatted off in the corner "with the other gals," on a Friday he managed to ask her, "Would you have a little spare time tonight to marry me at least?" After a trill of laughter, she said, "You're sweet," and let him walk her to her car. "This isn't marriage, but it's a start," he said cleverly, taking her by the hand. "May I kiss you?" "No," she answered.

On a Tuesday he notified her, whispering behind her ear when the group stood taking a breather, "I'm going to win you over. I'm going to break my heart like cracking an egg on the top of your head." While he had no idea himself where that poetic eruption came from, or its logic, she seemed impressed, turning around, smiling thoughtfully, and whispering back, "You *are* sweet." That night, as she went through the workout routine, he saw her as the model in the Elegancy Lingerie commercial, where in bra and panties she circles with ballroom ease through colonnades, across marble floors, invisible to an audience dressed in formal attire. Magically she becomes covered with a gleaming copper-sheen ball gown, dances on, her tall athletic form spinning the gown's billowy hem in airy whorls, and now everyone's eyes are indeed upon her, especially the man wearing a white dinner jacket and red cummerbund. Just as magically her coppery gown metamorphoses into a classic wedding dress, ivory, lacy, complete with matching veil. The man in the red cummerbund now is her dancing partner. She floats, a picture of what every bride should be.

When the class finished for the evening she said, "I want us to talk for a minute. I know a private spot." He followed her, both his spirit and his viscera afire over this lush turquoise figure leading him to "a private spot." They angled ahead, along a deserted corridor, where she halted by a drinking fountain.

One nifty foot placed forward, *pointe du pied*, her posture in textbook balance, she nevertheless seemed at a loss for words.

"Want me to talk first?" he asked.

She shook her head. "Listen, you're a nice fellow. Listen." Sighing, she checked around the vacant hallway that amplified their voices. "You like women who look like this, am I right?" And reaching up, she stretched out the neckline scoop of the turquoise leotard, dipping toward him so that inside he could see her pendant breasts, and beyond, down to her flat snowy stomach. "Am I right?"

"Uh. Yes?"

"You want to touch women there. Right?"

"Yes?"

"And, I do, too. Follow? Understand?"

He would, understand, he said, nodding many nods, courteously, and by attempting a defensive slurp from the nearby fountain he practically choked to death on a small sip of water.

iv

The Sunset Club had excellent racquetball courts, swimming pool, weight room, average meals in its dining hall, and a large bustling bar. In April he went there frequently and one night introduced himself to Rebecca, a haunting divorcée with a complex yet calm gaze, who would claim she was "close to" his age, although he guessed ten years older. Fine, he wanted a much older sophisticated woman. She was sitting alone at a bar table drinking a daiquiri, an elegant lady designed by nature and circumstance to glamorize instantly any social scene, her languid brown eyes raised above the rim of a cocktail glass sending out a thousand sympathies, or a thousand invitations.

He could imagine her with a cigarette, inhaling/exhaling smoke like it was a slow sexual act.

He bought her another daiquiri and they sat together, finding out about each other.

"Is anything wrong?" she asked.

"If I'm staring, that's a bad reflex I have with women."

"My, you don't sound happy about it."

He took a sip of his Manhattan. Shrugged.

"Tell me."

"I'll pass. No spoiling things for once."

"Do tell me. I want to hear." Her command had the authority of someone who intends to have her compassion taken seriously.

"Okay then. Okay, I'm thirty-three years old, still single, still waiting, so still looking. But I'm worn out from the looking."

She ordered her own Manhattan. "Listen to me, carefully," she said, applying what must be her considerable female intuition, "never give up. She's out there also searching. Believe me. 'Cause guess what? It's sort of a double scavenger hunt, with two people searching for someone else—each other—each one who got dropped or lost or left behind." Rebecca belonged on two highway billboards he had seen. One showed a man's face and a woman's companionable (and enraptured) face opposite his with a giant pilsner held between them, backlit so that the beer glowed gold with its foam top whiter than a cotton cloud. The second billboard focused on a faceted whiskey tumbler, half-filled with amber Kentucky Blend, circled by slim fingers with lengthy lavender nails, and held beside the face of a worldly lady whose enormous soulful eyes followed your every move as you drove past.

Her Manhattan refilled and mostly emptied, she reiterated her advice. "Never, never, give up. That's my message to you."

"I like hearing your message. Or your voice at least. The sound of it makes me tipsier than this booze."

"I learned everything there is to learn about giving up."

"From your former husband?"

"He lost patience with having to love me."

"I can't imagine it, any man leaving you. I can't."

"Oh, there aren't so many good marriages, as I judge it. Count how many you know of yourself. Go on. Not so easy, hmm. Give up?"

Scratching his head and his memory, he drank a stinger and she drank one. His best example, he finally told Rebecca, might be, he guessed, his brother's marriage, except his fumbled explanation had trouble pinpointing the reasons.

"The nights get endless," she asked, or was it a confession, "in bed by yourself?"

Those brave words startled him into believing—a leap of faith—it would be safe to speak, and trust her. "My nights. Miserable enough."

She sheltered him inside her voice, by simply saying, "Timmy, Timmy, Timmy."

Only Arlene had called him that before. And Rebecca's

voice was an enveloping force, sensual, husky, even hoarse, yet soothing, reminiscent of that Lauren Bacall actress from the old black-and-white movies. Rebecca's flawless facial bones did qualify her to be an actress or professional model, and she carried a veneer of dissipation, from having been handled by men, a use or abuse that underneath only sharpened her sensitivity and deepened her needs. On the outside, character lines may shadow those luminous eyes, while on the inside she remained virgin girl as much as scarred woman. Rebecca could play the film heroine who takes a war-fatigued soldier against her breast, cradles him, rocks him, crooning in her gravelly gentle tones, "Let's pull out of here, you and me. Travel off someplace far far away, the two of us, to a tiny village in a foreign country. We'll start over, be a couple of kids again. We could do whatever we want, anything, anything, like get married."

He bought Rebecca a Seagram's-on-the-rocks and suggested shifting to a secluded table, out of the commotion. She carried along a refill. Seated there, she caressed him with a rhythmic "Tim-my, Tim-my, how did the girls ever resist you?"

During their move, he had kept hold of her free hand. "I don't want a girl. I want a woman."

She finished the bourbon in a deliberate, programmatic, thoughtful way before rubbing one fingertip across the tips of his own fingers. "I enjoy touching your hand. It sends me a friendly warmth."

"And I feel your heat."

She rattled the ice cubes in her empty glass, which rang like wind chimes heard from inside a house. "Timothy, age thirty-three. Is that a rhyme? Timmy," she demanded, "I want you to kiss me."

Leaning across, he kissed her, lingeringly, full on the lips, detecting the mutual flavors of their liquor, tasting emotions more powerful than alcohol.

"You're not one of those damn girl-chasers," Rebecca said. "I can tell that, I can. I-can-I-can-I-can. You have something genuine to share with whatever woman you find to love."

"Your lips are velvet."

"Unless you already love Arlene."

"What?"

"You love her, don't you?"

"I think I love you."

"Tim-my . . ."

"I want to kiss you again," he said, "and after that again." They came together, Rebecca knocking over her glass, spilling the ice cubes, as they intertwined both hands.

Rebecca, fingers laced tightly into his, lifted his hands to blot or hide her brown eyes, now aglitter with tears. In the middle of this symbolic gesture, she trembled, untangled her fingers, bolted to her feet, anxious to hurry off. But she judged it was too late. Instead—in such a smooth sequence—she sank down again, snapped open her exquisite sequined evening purse, vomited into it, neatly, twice, and clicked the purse briskly shut. After an entire lifetime he could never erase this vignette that had lasted mere heartbeats: how proficient, and oddly, how graceful, she had been.

Rebecca said, "Very, very sorry. All I need is a little chaser to fix everything up."

"Let's not do that."

"*Yes.*"

"I won't, Rebecca."

Wet eyes addressing him directly, she pronounced in that magnificent throaty voice, muffled by a napkin pressed against her mouth, similar to hiding a broken tooth, "You can go. He didn't care to watch either. He, my husband. I don't blame him, don't blame you." However, 33-year-old Timothy obeyed his gentleman's instincts, refusing to rush away. Out of a consideration that combined as much affection as pity, he bought her another bourbon. When he did begin his goodbyes, she broke in, "This is embarrassing. Do you have a few extra bucks? I'm short tonight."

V

In June he was alone with Arlene in his brother's apartment, helping clean the day's dishes, their standard Saturday group routine while waiting for Conrad's return from a weekend work shift. It happened she flicked soap suds at him, a Saturday game of her own. Following the script he flicked a towel back. It happened she hit him two playful jabs in the ribs, launching a third, and he tickled her in self-defense, and it happened he swung her around, running his hands under her blouse and kissing her forcefully enough on the mouth that Arlene let out a yelp, from pain and surprise.

"Why on earth did you do that?" she gasped, blouse drooping from her waistband.

"No idea."

"No idea?"

"No idea. Just wanted to hear what you'd say?"

"I don't know what to say."

"Perfect then. Perfect answer." He retreated to the television set, switching channels in a loop of distraction.

"Timmy?" Arlene moved back nearer to him, in half-steps nearer yet, having tucked in her blouse. "And what was I supposed to say. What did you want me to say?"

"I didn't *want* you to say anything, silly."

"But Timmy. And I'm not silly."

"I know you're not. But wake up, it's Saturday and past time for you to haul out that Bissell and finish wearing your carpets down to fur balls."

She gathered herself in a pause of stock-still silence before saying, softly, "That's mean. You don't like me, really."

His head flinched sideways, and downward, away from the television, without looking, quite, at her. "Jesus. Jesus Christ." In a few minutes he heard the vacuum motor humming, off in a bedroom, the humming accented by unusually careless thumps against furniture. A few more minutes and the vacuum cleaner died off in a decrescendo whine.

Arlene marched a deliberate path to his side. "I need you to tell me. Timmy, what did you hope I'd say?"

"Please stop asking me. Please."

"I will ask. I am asking. I'll keep asking."

This forced finale required coming to his feet, turning, straightening his shoulders and stiffening his backbone, his face focused over her face. "Arlene, here's the setup. Here's our agreement. If I tell you, afterward never mention these things again, never, and let me go back to being a brother-in-law. Agreed?"

She blinked with a tremor of eyelashes, an action that punished him as always with the sensational picture of those blue eyes, one being noticeably deeper blue than the other. She nodded, or apparently nodded, blinking again her blue and bluer eyes—an anatomical stutter. "Maybe I agree, that is. Maybe."

"Oh, no, no, no. No maybe about it."

Now she did, in fact, stutter. "Ss-ooo. I should stick, I think, to maybe I will agree."

"*No* maybe."

"Then maybe no maybe."

The Sum of All My Parts

Who out in the wide world cares much about this Beth&Wally? Honestly, nobody does. These two were born to be ignored. The question's more important variant is, do Beth and Wally care about Beth&Wally?

Elizabeth and Wallace (but never thus called) live in a tiny house in a rural burg with the accurate if unimaginative name of Farmersville, lost in the ravenous space of California's San Joaquin Valley. Wally is short and thin and Beth looks half his size.

Today a stern August sun heads down behind dusty cottonwood trees, the windless leaves like dog tongues locked in a pant, while inside their little house Beth and Wally eat a little and talk a little about little things. Finally the reluctant sun throws its farewell light across the colossal pewter sky, although Beth and Wally seldom notice sunsets.

As night arrives and they prepare to sleep—putting their clothes away in a closet that uses a total of only eleven hangers—where are the people who should care about Beth and Wally, such as their parents? Chiefly dead, the parents, by the usual villains: two mothers from cigarettes, one father from booze. The other father is in either Colorado, Texas, or Florida, or after three years of silence, could be dead himself—a clean sweep. Siblings? They have none. Children? None. Friends? Probably all the official 616 folks of Farmersville, which is to say, none.

Beth and Wally pull up the covers, lying there in the dark, in their doll house, in a studio bed that they never realize was designed for a single body.

*****

It was not love at first or second sight. Beth and Wally got married as a predictable result of their genetic fates, and of course, their proximity in Farmersville. With the meager social game that is Farmersville, they were the last two left standing, unchosen on the sidelines, when the marital teams were picked to play.

Weighing under 130 pounds, shaped like a stick, Wally to this day resembles a teenage stripling, one who has managed to put drooping age lines under and around his sleepy eyes. His gait is always sauntering, slow, and his speech likewise, slow, often running out of vocabulary altogether. For this reason, and a few others, the townspeople judge Wally to be well over on the dim side, but a check into his confidential school or Army files would reveal an IQ close to his body temperature. He is the first to admit that he was never clever, never at ease, when forced into the analytical. He dropped from high school during his third year as much to escape the classroom as to take a job at the cotton gin and earn dollars for his sick and needy family.

After his big accident in the Army, Wally returned to Farmersville with a modest disability pension and found a job stocking shelves and sweeping floors at the hardware store, where over the years he became as familiar a product of the inventory as its shovels and dog food. He is not unhappy there.

Three short blocks away from Phillip's Farm Center—the hardware store—Beth works mornings tallying weight receipts for the local truck scale, and has faithfully done this since graduating high school. Behind a bruised hulking desk built circa 1930 that showed and even smelled its age, she sits in a swivel chair on a stack of cushions. At several inches shorter than five feet Beth is smaller than petite, small enough to have suffered a childhood of dwarf taunts, while as an adult she never grew much either, having negligible hips and breasts the size of baseballs. To be direct about it, Beth is considered plain. The unkindly in Farmersville might say less than plain. As compensation she does have a lavish mound of wavy chestnut hair, and a gentle nature. All would agree with that.

Beth has always been, as the simile goes, "Smart as a whip," but given her insecurities, a whip very infrequently cracked in the open air for anyone to hear. Way back in fourth grade kind Mrs. Pferde had perceived this brightness and told her "Honeybunch, you're precious enough to put in my pocket and take straight home." What Beth heard, however, was less the compliment and more just another remark about being a runty kid.

It would be hard to determine exactly how the Beth&Wally marriage ever came to happen—that is, the specific courtship steps of it. Certainly nobody in nosy Farmersville saw the typical signs or signals, although Beth and Wally were known to be the only two people who ate bag lunches at the weedy town park. This park circlet had three unpainted wooden benches lined up together inside a gravel patch, with a half-dozen trees, abandoned landscaping, and a drinking fountain that functioned. A reasonable assumption could be that at a certain point it became impossible for Beth and Wally to keep ignoring each other. And yes, as the noon hours came and went, they were eventually seen on the same park bench, eating from their paper bags, talking. It was the middle bench, conveniently closest to the drinking fountain, the one in front of a WWI bronze memorial plaque hiding under an oleander.

When they first kissed—a tentative bump of lips and teeth—the place and time were the opposite of the public park, occurring instead in the moonless dark of a sandy side street where Beth rented a room. "That was my first kiss," Beth said afterward, this given as observation, not any confession. They had stood in the darkness while Wally gathered his thoughts.

"Mine, too," he said at last, thereby proving that both of them, without perceiving it, lacked all defensive skills or even the instinct for saving face.

Neither Wally—nor Beth—had "declared love" or "proposed marriage" in the storybook sense. They just fumbled along a natural downslope path leading to the necessary documents. Beth used her experience with paperwork. For a laughably cheap price they bought the house that nobody else wanted, one hammered together by a weekend carpenter who forced, somehow, five rooms inside less that 500 square feet. Beth&Wally moved in, a married couple.

*****

Even a simple life has a few complexities. And commonplace Beth&Wally have two that they share.

The first unexpected story is from Beth, who has brought a *miracle* into their miniature home, to borrow the term used by her obstetrician. After almost fifteen years of marriage she is pregnant. Her childlike body, formerly so unworthy of distinction or praise, is now suddenly curving into an exotic shape. Mornings, while dressing herself, evenings, when undressing, Beth finds some minutes in their cubicle bathroom to rise up on tiptoes and study the mirror's reflection. "Okay," she thinks, "that's me. That's Beth." She rotates the image from full-front to profile right, to profile left, and reverses the order of poses. "That's Elizabeth." Her breasts have gotten tender. The breasts, she is certain, have grown.

And recently new confirmation of Beth's miracle has arrived, inescapable as Beth and Wally press together in their comically narrow bed. They both can feel the jolt of baby life shifting and poking up against Beth's skin. When the movement happens Beth and Wally, quite silent, remain motionless for long afterward, absorbing in perplexed fashion the presence of this third person under the crowded sheets with them.

Beth and Wally never discuss the significance or consequence of having a child, the weight of the subject being beyond their conversational habits. They behave more like novice spectators seated, almost trapped, in the front row of a huge amphitheater, waiting for the first act of a famous drama to begin.

Wally's own mystery is far less traditional than Beth's pregnancy. Granted, it could never be called traditional in the least.

A stranger might wonder why Wally always forgets to shake an outstretched hand. Or someone might notice how Wally puts on his coat with a series of fidgety hitches. Ultimately people do see that Wally is missing his right hand. Yet the mystery is not the missing hand. That misfortune can be seen elsewhere, with others. The unexpected—the genuine surprise—comes from the fact that his hand is not altogether missing, because Wally has the lost hand pickled in a glass jar, and keeps it close by, on top of the bedroom dresser at home, under a table lamp. In no way is this the familiar memorabilia of saving cute baby teeth, or a sentimental snippet of childhood hair, or the pebble art of a gallstone, or even the joke of a worthless appendix. There in the jar by their bed is a perfect human hand, floating in formaldehyde, fingernails tapping against the glass. Wally may not look at the hand for a solid month. He may look at it every day for a month straight. If he has a second cup of strong coffee for dinner, in the middle of the night he may switch on the lamp.

*****

Beth has known the history of this companion hand from the start, back during those lunchtime hours at the park when Wally finally told her, "I have a special thing at home, a part of me that's off of me but not away from me and keeps being my part." Beth had been astonished. Not shocked, she was only amazed, somehow even enchanted. Because she had just discovered another Wally, the one who when talking to her about the hand turned pink in the face with intensity, whose eyes sharpened with sincerity, and who—hard for outsiders to have believed—spoke with the flair if not the vocabulary of a poetic mind. From that point on, Beth took equal possession of the hand's importance, due to what it meant, and did, to Wally. Although in their general poverty they had no pets to share their lives, no hobbies for amusements, no money certainly to buy indulgences, no goals to chase with dreams, they did have together their own remarkable jar over there on a white crocheted doily atop their bedroom dresser.

Beth is always ready to hear once more the tale about the

hand, and on occasion prompts the telling with a freshly phrased question, any trivial one serving the purpose. "What anyway was the weather? Who then was with you? Did you faint? Were you scared? Could you speak?" Beth already knows the basic answers, but she also knows that Wally will tumble into enough inspiration to make his answers original, make new vocal scenes more alive than any rote recitations of worn yesteryear memories. This is why Beth listens, and watches, carefully.

That fateful afternoon occurred in the Army, a place where Wally gratefully would have settled into a career. The Army fed him, clothed him, provided a roof to live under, checked over his health, would promote him to sergeant with an early retirement. "But it wasn't meant to turn out thataway," says Wally. "That morning there in the barracks, shaving, what did I never guess about anything different. I *should* have talked to that hand, my right hand, holding the razor and zipping around on my face like it had a brain of its own. Maybe I *should've* given the hand a big thank-you. 'I appreciate you. Look at you go. What a terrific job. Thank you, sir.' But I never ever even guessed. Turns out I was eyeballing its final movie show that morning."

And the weather. "Summer hot. Middle of the afternoon, close to 3:00. Beautiful blue shiny sky, by the way. Well, we have our shirts off, 'cause lots of sweat from loading pallets at the depot yard. My arm rests against a pallet. I'm listening to my partner talk, name of Bruenner, a corporal from

Milwaukee city. The whole business is about to go boom-boom-BOOM. This guy on the forklift takes no attention of how we stood there on a break. His forklift rams the pallet too hard. The metal band that wraps the pallet load—sharp as your sharpest kitchen knife, Beth—twists and snaps and whistles like a monster spring coming unwound. *Whizz.* My hand's there, just right, just wrong, whatever. 1-2-3 the hand's gone, chopped clean off. Blood squirts out like a broke garden hose. Lucky for me Bruenner has a real fast head and fast fingers. Good old Bruenner reaches down, squeezes off the blood, and he saves my life."

Wally had a storehouse of sensory details to retrieve, almost microscopic in their particulars, describing how "puny" the blow had felt, no harder than when once in sixth grade "a teacher slapped me on the wrist for nodding off in class," yet powerful enough to slice through bone. Wally could recreate the colors for Beth, such as the "thick red" arc of healthy blood against that "blue blue" sky, reminding him of those "simple deep colors that kindergarten kids pick out for painting." There was the image of his actual hand down on the gravel by itself, "which made no sense at all. What's going on here, I keep asking myself, did some dumb somebody pull a dumb clown stunt with a dumb rubber hand?" And, yes, he could talk, sort of, and no he "didn't black out," although he "got sleepy" and Bruenner shouted into his ear every minute or so. As their jeep raced to the hospital and while the pokey landscape seemed anyhow in no hurry to pass by, Wally had examined the "funniness" of Bruenner's fingers "being disappeared under my blood, like a buddy amputee" and Wally was hearing his own faraway voice apologizing "Sorry 'bout your pants" and later the same voice repeating "Sorry 'bout your pants. I'll buy . . ." And Bruenner had interrupted, "Shut the shit up about my pants. When we get through with this I'm buying new duds for both of us."

His days in the hospital had stayed adrift until hearing a thoughtless comment from an orderly: "Hey guy, imagine what. Your hand's still here somewheres in the building. The docs was, well, for awhile, the docs was playing with an idea of sewing it back on again." Wally wasted not a second, telling the orderly, "You look to me like a fella who wants to get rich." Not rich exactly, but the orderly did want the $1033 cash that Wally had saved up at the bank.

So his hand was smuggled out, pickled in a clean super-sized mayonnaise jar from the mess hall. To store the jar until his release from the hospital and the Army, Wally asked Corporal Bruenner for help, who inhaled a stiff drag on a Lucky Strike, squinted, nodded consent, and said, "Got more enterprise than you let on, ain't you, you little squirt." Bruenner never asked why about anything and Wally never needed to explain or justify. Wally had reclaimed what was his own. He refused the Army's offer (an insistence, practically) to be fitted for a prosthesis. "Thanks but no thanks." Wally already had his real hand back.

Thereafter the jar and its hand never moved far out of

Wally's sight or out of his reach. Nothing ever changed about the hand, with its same calluses, same bony knuckles, same tendons branching below those knuckles, likewise his branching veins, his dark hair in wet ringlets, his same two moles nestled together at the fork of the thumb, even the dirt under his fingernails despite the limitless bath did not wash away—altogether every single piece staying the same, Wally would point out to Beth. "You see. Nothing different." She would agree, most emphatically. By placing Wally's left hand alongside the jar, in an identical upright position, the two hands formed an obvious twinned set. The squared cuticles, the tapered fingers with lengthy third segments, the thin wrists, each component a true match, brother-to-brother, and Wally would say, "Like in a mirror," and Beth would add, "Like in a mirror, completely."

For months after the accident, many months, there remained for Wally a genuine connection to his absent hand that few people could conceive. In bed, with Wally waiting for sleep, under the covers his right hand was suddenly *there*, twitching, sending stinging signals up its arm. In the blackness he could feel the *weight* of the hand insisting on its presence—what the doctors named "phantom nerves"— all convincing enough that Wally had to investigate with his left hand and touch the empty space to disprove the lie. Often he would then swing his legs from the bed, sit up, lean over, feel for the slick glass, turn on the nearby lamp. Give the jar a brisk shake and the hand inside spins, waves hello, rises under the momentum to strike the lid, testing the passage out. Wally has the strength with his left hand to lift that heavy mayonnaise jar against the bare bulb, gazing like a clairvoyant gypsy into an Andalusian crystal globe.

What Wally reads in front of him is his autobiography, only better than words on the paper of a diary, because here is the actual participant in the flesh. Take that silver scar there across the base of his thumb, from a nasty bicycle crash when he was eight. His mother had been more upset than Wally, cupping his gashed right hand between her own two, and you betcha, Corporal Bruenner, hers got bloody, same as yours. "Wally, Wally," she had shrilled, "we'll hurry you to the doctor." Had he foreseen both their futures, he would have told his mother, "Forget my hand. Let's use the money and ask the doctor instead why you cough and spit up every night."

His mother had held this hand often over the childhood years, his father but once, at least that Wally remembers. He had called his only child Wally aside, grabbed Wally's right hand, fumbling, making a botch of it, and announced in a tired monotone, "My liver's supposed to kill me by December." His father always skipped ahead to the main point. Turned out, his father lingered for two Decembers more, to everybody's regret, especially his. Wally was at the Bakersfield hospital when his father officially died, watching that stack of bones sleep, until a nurse came in and said, nope, sleep it wasn't.

Wally at times wonders, as he looks into the jar, is it correct what he hears, that those fingertip whorls are different from anyone else's on the entire planet. Or does that mean even in all the heavens?

*****

It is before noon when Beth leaves work early and comes home, a great rarity for her. But she feels a shadow passing through her body—Beth describes the sensation to herself this way—and she wants to be alone. At the house Beth begins planning a strangely elaborate lunch meal, banging pots and pans down from the cupboard, putting some back, lining up mismatched ingredients from the pantry and refrigerator, putting some back, flipping through her recipe file, starting a song and stopping and starting it again because she apparently knows only half the chorus, which bothers her.

Or what bothers her is that twinge. Was it in fact a twinge, down there, located at the center of her miracle? And was it the first or second twinge?

Beth forgets today's lunch, switches to memorizing a menu for tonight's dinner, and then tomorrow's lunch and tomorrow's dinner. She locks her concentration on the perfect spices for a tasty pork roast (brown sugar/mustard/pepper rub) and the vinaigrette oil for her homemade salad dressing (sour cream/ garlic clove/three tablespoons of lemon juice) and how about possibly Wally's special favorite, a pumpkin pie (cinnamon/ ginger/nutmeg/shredded almond sprinkles on top).

Except trouble is coming, has already arrived. The third twinge or fourth, or however many the number, can only be a stabbing cramp, no pretending otherwise. Beth leaves the kitchen to lie on the bed. With a hand spread against her belly she waits for the baby to move. Beth is a patient person and she waits and waits. When the cramping forces her back up on her feet she shifts into the bathroom, lifting her dress to see a trail of blood, no wider than one of her knitting needles, meandering its lazy garish path down the inside of her pale thigh.

Beth shakes her head at her own hipless, boyish body in the mirror, as if scolding it: "I never did trust you. Never, never. My whole life I never believed you could do any one single thing properly."

Doubled forward now from the pain, Beth understands that today is going to end in sadness, and end soon, and she pushes herself through their box of a house, at last finding the vintage camera Wally uses every Christmas. Its back is open, without film. For the first time on this day Beth lets out a moan, for her dearest wish is to take a picture, a photograph and a keepsake of the baby girl, no matter how unpleasant a lifeless object she might appear to the rest of the world.

When Wally arrived at the medical clinic he recalls that he has never seen Beth cry—not even now is she—but behind that ruffled curtain of chestnut hair her face is blotchy, her puffy eyes are red, and he speculates that crying has gone on somewhere, sometime, not long ago.

Not long ago.

*****

Another August sunset has finished. On their first night back home together Beth&Wally are sitting on their little bed in their little house. And since the house is little Beth has an immediate question.

"You switched the jar around, did you?"

Wally's tilt sideways suggests an answer.

"And where then?" Beth scans the room, knowing the jar will be near.

"No, no," says Wally, "not here. I dropped the jar inside Johnson's dry well, in his back pasture, that old well with the wood cover, you remember. It was dry, for darn sure. I heard glass break down at the bottom."

Beth has no words to speak. Simply no words. Eventually she does manage to ask the obvious, the *why*.

Wally jiggles a shoulder.

The tiny house shrinks tighter and tighter with the silence between Beth&Wally. Scrunched there side-by-side on their ridiculous bed, Beth&Wally are already pushed as close as close can be made.

Mrs. Pferde proves herself perceptive, once again, all these many years later. Honeybunch Beth is precious enough to put into your pocket and wise enough to figure out the score. Beth picks up Wally's hand and pats it, strokes it. She says, "I do know why now."

Wally collects his ideas for a response, which perhaps will reach his tongue a bit later, or not. Meanwhile he takes the initiative and turns Beth's hand over, holding it, caressing the palm simultaneously, meaning for Wally that he uses a solo thumb for double duty. No special trick required. Just an old skill Wally had to learn.

My Name Is Santa Claus

Most likely you won't believe me. Fair enough. People seldom do (the young children excepted) when introduced to me in the flesh. Santa. Claus. Still it's true. Bizarre, absurd, for certain, yet true, and if you ask how it could happen I have no real answer.

As crude fact, my paternal grandparents immigrated from Bavaria with the familial handle of *Claus* already attached, and I was born near my mother's favorite New Mexico city of *Santa* Fe. But please. Both these clumsy details allow no sensible excuse. When as a teenager I reached an age to question properly about their decision, my parents had already disappeared together on that sad flight #55 of Northern Airways, along with eighty-eight other strangers.

Explanations? Unlikely that my parents can be dismissed as clueless fools, each having earned not one but two degrees from a very proud American university. Nor were they hasty in this naming business. Inside a shoebox holding only a pathetic pinch of childhood documents, I found a disproportionate *three* reminders from the County of Santa Fe, asking for the full name of the new baby boy to record legally his birth certificate.

Also neither parent left any—or rather any other—known evidence of silliness. My mother on the contrary, I have heard, was serious to a fault, burdening herself and friends with frequent stubborn hours of "spiritual concentration." Sometimes in the vacant sections of the late late night, when the mind goes adrift toward the profound, I almost wonder whether she was sensing, or at least wishing, an otherworldly vision about her son which he is too thick-witted to comprehend. Of course in the morning's light I know this is quite foolish.

I admit never once considering a formal change of name. Never, never. Indeed I allow it—alongside the complete address—to be printed in public places for the whole world to view. Changing my name seems outright dangerous, altering the single step in history that could trip up everybody else afterward into an unintended jumble. A change, furthermore, frankly, feels disrespectful or disloyal, especially to those two people we call Mother and Father. By the way, photographs of my parents resemble their only child utterly not the slightest.

Tales of hospital babies being switched come to mind.

So what is, is. Nothing gained, really, by my graphically revealing here a lifetime of predictable schoolyard teasing, of snorts and snickers, of the constant eruption of quizzical eyebrows. Et cetera. Ad absurdum. No, what matters now can only be that I am what I am named.

What has this fate brought to me? Torment and enrichment, let us say. With the first half, I, Mr. Santa Claus, exist as nothing more than helpless mental ether, given solid form solely by the needy. With the second half I receive more substance than I would ever earn on my feeble own. Unbelievable how I hear from every point on the human compass, from the small and the even smaller, from the weak and even weaker, from future angels and from the insane. I answer them, each of them when they write, always, eventually.

Now, do you want to hear the authentically crazy? Then here is what I should *not* tell, except I will, since how can any fantastical claim of mine be completely unacceptable after we have already jumped together across the dizzy threshold of nonsense. Nonetheless, hold on tight. My written answers, that I return, I can only give to actual letters, real correspondence with words on real paper. Because the process starts when I hold their envelopes in my hands. With an index finger and thumb I feel across the stamp surface and along the envelope edges, tracing the tingle of the person who touched there before me. Carefully, I pull up the flap if possible, hoping to expose the glue where a tongue has licked. From certain effervescent molecules a unique scent arises, different envelope to envelope. I breathe it, deeply, sniffing like a hound dog on the hunting trail. The writing in the letter itself interests me at first merely as obscure swirls of hieroglyphics, tactile designs without direct translation but with a definite narrative to tell, as if chiseled on paper stone, instead of being embossed linen stationery or smudged notepad or a reversed scrap of last year's Christmas wrapping. Lastly I do read the letter. With my fingernails, so to speak, I peel back the skin from every hopeful word, probing for the raw meat of truth. Unavoidably some bleeding takes place to both parties in this procedure.

There sits the letter on my desk. I sit, too. In difficult cases this exchange between us can last hours. But wait I must, and wait more, because there will arrive—collecting itself into perfection like the wonder of a snow crystal—a clear face with an entire exact story. I do not lie. The whole experience still scares me to be honest. And continuing with honesty, I did lie about that dream of my mother's supernatural vision of her son. In the mornings I never believe it is foolishness.

In the farthest reaches of my imagination, or in its darkest regions, I accuse my parents of lovingly, cruelly, deliberately turning me into an orphan as preparation for the life I lead. For while much happiness and purpose arise from my annual actions, that same generous promise to others deals a trial to the soul. Dear Mother, dear Father, you were right, so very right, to train me for future tribulations, although I thank you for your sacrifice without ever forgiving your departure.

Does anyone care to learn about this uninvited hurt that visits me every season? If yes, dear Mother, dear Father, dear Anyone, then you have permission to read the confidential messages that follow, grabbed almost at random from a recent file in a locked cabinet labeled THE EMPEROR OF NO.

Forgive me for neglecting to weed out the failed partial messages and practice drafts. I just hate revisiting that cabinet.

****

Dear Ms. Leblanc:

What a kind (if puzzling) letter and if only I had a spare minute, certainly I'd attempt to solve that puzzle. Regrettably, as the world reminds me, 'Tis the Season, and can you imagine how many nervous youngsters are chewing their fingertips right now?

*

Dear Ms. Leblanc:

Pardon?

*

Dear Bobby:

Doing chores is fine. But to write "breaking my butt" is uncivil. 9-year-old boys don't mail off sentences about butts, nor, by the bye, should they write "F**KY DUCKY" in red crayon on the taxpayers' hallway floor at Graceland Elementary School, although sometimes such boys do end up with red butts. Discuss this with your father when you unwrap your ten-speed box of dried fruit.

*

Dear Nadine:

Could not read your handwriting, darling. Sorry. Maybe next year. Ask Miss Starch to work with you especially on m's, n's, l's, t's, and letters that go below the line.

*

Dear Jonah:

The postage-due situation has gotten flat out of hand. You'd be surprised how much it hurts us up here, Jonah. Yours was one of many careless letters on that score. Accordingly, everybody must suffer a smidgen, as *for instance* by being satisfied with a single-battery thingamabob instead of a double. In the meantime search under the sofa cushions and find a few pennies for a stamp.

*

Dear Ms. Leblanc:

Your questions mystify me. Yes, of course, I've visited Cracklebee, Louisiana, but your cryptic allusions—"spilled Chardonnay," "blue lights," "5-foot 10-inch woman," etc.— have me stumped. Mistaken identity, don't you suppose? Better luck elsewhere.

*

Liebe Kristina!

Du würdest Mutti ein

Oops, wrong language, Christine. How thoughtful of you to write about your mommy instead of yourself. All in all, you're the best girl on your block, and among the top half-dozen girls in your whole town. That ain't peanuts, Christine. Good going. *Unfortunately*, a mother *can* be peanuts, as you'll figure out during the next four or five years. Or specifically, sweetheart, it's what your mommy keeps hidden in an empty peanut jar on an upper shelf in the kitchen that's the trouble, and why I won't put sharp objects in her hands.

Let's think about embroidered hankies and, mainly, let's think about Christine.

*

Dear Giletta:

I believe you forgot a couple of phrases from that song. "Better not pout" belongs in there, too. The scene you perform every Saturday is a scandal. Some friendly advice: (a) Make your bed. (b) Pick up your (currently) 16 pieces of littered laundry. (c) Smile while so doing. (d) Clean the floor. Your very own Junior Carpet Sweeper might help. (I picked out your special color, Pretty Princess Pink.)

*

Dear Ms. Leblanc:

Let's say, as a 100% rhetorical hypothesis, that on a particularly famous evening a strange man abruptly appeared in a certain house, its darkness lit by a small string of blue ceremonial bulbs, when behold, he bumps into the female occupant, and an erotic accident occurs betwixt them. What would this represent, in practical fact. Not so much.

A moment of total surprise, almost a moment of total confusion, the murky shapes and faces, the voicelessness—all these contain an insular motive, better off without identities, daylight, or words. Instead its magic comes from the nightfall, the surreal blue skin with black hollows, the elusive brevity, don't you think? And as such, let's agree, the scene is best preserved, in the season's peaceful spirit, when partly forgotten rather than fully recalled.

*

Dear Henry (Hank):

No can do. Sit down for a minute and think about it.

*

Dear Ramona:

Sweetie, they just don't make those things to fit 6-year-old girls, as a rule. A Smarty Pants doll instead, exactly like you, has more upstairs than up front.

*

Dear Alice:

You must be responsible for your actions, Alice. You shove Tabby into the freezer. You slam the door. You leave and leave and leave him inside. You give poor Tabby brain damage. He ruins $300 of good food. Kitty has to be put "to sleep." No, Alice.

*

Dear Ms. Leblanc:

The greatest gifts can truly be given but once, if you reflect on it. Thereafter they become lasting heirlooms, inherited from your jewelry chest or your memory, mainly the latter. We should rejoice in whatever blessings already came our lucky way!

*

Dear Martin:

October 11th, Monday afternoon, after school, rain puddles on the street, someone smaller than you has his face down in the mud—some genuinely nice kid has his face being pushed down in the mud. Enough said, Martin?

Wait, Martin, know what'd be a ding-dong terrific idea? For you, Martin? Grab two slices of fresh Honey Bunny white bread (that soft stuff you like so much), spread them an inch thick with butter and gooey sweet strawberry jam, and then cram the sandwich straight up your nose.

*

Dear LizAnn:

I'll second the motion: Having three older brothers is having about three too many. But I can't legally ship them away. What we need to do is either wait for you to grow bigger or them to shrink. Check back with me in four years and we'll decide which. Meanwhile, eat plenty of protein.

*

Dear Myra:

*

Dear Bruce:

So much refined sugar would dissolve your tongue, or if not that, your colon. (Look the last word up in a dictionary.) Substitution: Tofu bars with carob sprinkles. Mmmm.

*

Dear Myra:

Myra, Myra, dear Myra

*

Dear Ms. Leblanc:

I admire a statuesque woman, with her lanky strong thighs, those wide lean hips, broad shoulders, long hair down a long passionate back, long feet, long supple fingers. For some reason, possibly environmental, many of our office folk around here stay kind of stubby. And my favorite color does happen to be twilight blue, the shade a notch under pure purple. That combination (to finish up a strictly abstract admission) would be deadly for me—a tall swaying lady, as sensuous as a pine in the wind, surrounded by haunting blue lights in a black room.

*

Dear Myra:

Where to start, Myra, where to start. Where.

*

Dear Ms. Leblanc:

You complain about "muggy Louisiana nights" and loneliness. Many and various are the landscapes for loneliness, Ms. Leblanc. Consider, if you will, scenery of an absolute whiteness, such as a vast searing New Mexico desert, or its mirror image, an immense arctic wasteland. Have you ever read a chapter titled "The Whiteness of the Whale" in that Moby Dick book? No? Just let me jot down some sentences from my mother's old copy, words she underlined and probably left for me to find. "In essence whiteness is not so much a color as the visible absence of color, and at the same time the concrete of all colors; is it for these reasons that there is such a dumb blankness, full of meaning, in a wide landscape of snows . . . from which we shrink?"

I'll ask you, Ms. Leblanc, to imagine living with such a visual chill for as far as the eye can roam, with bleak vistas of ice, their glassy monotony, invisible winds sliding across the void, and temperatures that would freeze the earlobes off a brass monkey. And then, Ms. Leblanc, then, comes an entire season of sundown. Imagine *that*, please. The circumstances up here (a monumental irony) often are saturnine, not to say morbid. People have been known to, or been driven to, apply facial cosmetics in an attempt at portraying good health and good cheer. For persons like these, Louisiana must be a paradise, so sultry is it, so vernal, a place where you don't need to bundle up around the clock, where you can literally see flesh and the contours of bodies through skimpy clothing of every sort. Why, you're blessed, Ms. Leblanc, to dwell in a land of sweaty bare skin.

*

Dear Myra:

*

Dear Ms. Leblanc:

Fair is fair. Your maroon satin bathrobe received a slight

separation at the shoulder stitching, almost a year ago now, and why don't we replace it with new nightwear—a soft velour nightshirt with side slits, for example. Or how about a halter top and hip-hugger pajama pants, cut below the navel. Or a backless caftan. Or a shimmery blue/black tricot nylon jumpsuit, tight at the top, tight at the crotch, tight at the bottom. Or a mini wrap, made of silk gauze, sans sash.

"Which should it be?" you ask.

"Try them on, one by one," I reply.

"How's this?" you ask, with the first.

"Go before the window, over there. Let the moon shine through the fabric. Now the next."

"And this one?" You twirl, girlish, delighted.

"Let me feel the material. What's that perfect scent on your hair?"

"Only my hair."

"It reminds me of magnolia leaves. It reminds me of standing in the sun."

"Here. Nuzzle me, snuggle."

"My gracious. I tore your sleeve again."

"That means you'll bring another nightgown, next year."

"This cycle could continue without end. We'd have an eternity of torn seams."

"Promise we will, promise me, promise, promise. I deserve it, don't I?"

"Except, do I?"

*

Dear Carl:

There are OK places to pee and places not OK. Mrs. Bennett had worked hard all spring on her lawn. You saw her working hard. She very much wanted the dichondra to be green and nice when her sister flew all the way from Connecticut to visit on the 4th of July. As Mrs. Bennett told you once, she hadn't seen her sister for over seven years. Mrs. Bennett felt quite disappointed. Her sister was disappointed that Mrs. Bennett felt disappointed. I was disappointed. And here comes your turn.

*

Dear Myra:

Dear little Myra. Thank you for enclosing your photograph. You're a charmer and you can never ever know how

*

Dear Ms. Leblanc:

I concur. I'm a man, "very human," as you express it. Sure I could be unpredictable, be downright daring. Sure I could conjure us together in a different season and at a daylight hour. Let's go for square in the middle of a summer afternoon, thusly:

> *And tall within the open door,*
> *As sunlight entered*
> *Painting both lady and floor,*
> *Ms. Leblanc smiled, and it*

Became impossible to tell
Any bright difference between
Where sun and smile fell.

See, I did conceive of it.

*

Dear Lanette:

Yep, indeedy, Uncle Felix promised to build you a corral behind his condo if you got a pony. But I don't believe the city of Minneapolis allows a horse in his parking space, and actually, Uncle Felix never dreamed you might turn up with the real object. Uncles sometimes say way too much just to make nieces happy.

Take it from me (who owns eight—no, nine—head of livestock), real cows or ponies, or such, eat mountains of expensive hay and grain, and cleaning out the stables is a yucky chore. HOWEVER, another fuzzy, friendly, toy pony would be super. An Appaloosa? It can sleep right in the bedroom with you and your others. What a big herd you'll have!

*

Dear Ms. Leblanc:

You wait in the blackness of your living room, at the one spot, due to the chance placement of a loop of blue bulbs, that permits your hair, your shoulders, hips, legs, to be silhouetted in continuous curves. The time: the hour following midnight,

I think. Anyway, my finicky watch with a will of its own has been stuck at that point on the dial for ages.

I appear and it happens. You give a short gasp, startled at my suddenness, and amazed, despite your preparations, at the actual sight of me. I move closer to calm you. You put forth your hands, either to defend yourself or to welcome me, but as our hands join, we both smile, in tandem, helplessly. The new blue that glistens in the dark is your rising tears. Your low voice tries to speak—sounding more than anything like a stifled ache—and for silence I press my finger vertically against my lips and next horizontally, with another meaning, gently against yours. Then, what I never planned, you kiss my finger back.

Our temples touch as we lean together, for we are the same height, and we make a single shadow in a room too dim for two shadows. Even in this shadowiness we feel more substantial than before. At least I do, because to live as a caricature is scarcely to exist, and Ms. Leblanc, your clinging body, with mine, together, construct a most tangible privacy, not my usual vaporous public performance.

We inhale our secretive atmosphere. We stand, your hands locked behind my collar, mine behind your waist, while we sway in our own invented dance, following our own heartbeat rhythm. You tip back your face. You have an arcing neck fit for a Nefertiti. The one teardrop on each cheek is from happiness, you claim. I taste them, erase them. And I

*

Dear Howard (Howie):

What luck. You already take presents from stores without paying for them. Now nobody needs to worry about buying you a costly Hang Ten skateboard or a WarpSpeed Video Gamester.

*

Dear Ms. Leblanc:

I'm weak at the joints. I'm an easy crippled target. Your letter caught me at this vulnerable period, in the depths of the dozen days I most dread—namely, my annual final review of rejections. During these twelve endless, vicious days I call myself The Emperor of No.

Did I say dread? And loathe. I dread and loathe these days, dread and loathe my own self. How can I do this. How, when even the worst kindergarten hoodlums have small hearts that break, when even the tiniest misanthropes weep a lot.

It turned my hair silver years ago. No joke.

Certainly I do tell myself the customary arguments and rationales, such as the maxim that goes, approximately, "They shall learn right only through the lesson of wrong, discover pleasure only by the example of pain." But you and I each understand, Ms. Leblanc, that what is wanted here, for them, in their fumbled lives, is not instruction, not proof of common sense or common decency, but outrageous, benevolent fantasy, the world's last secure refuge.

Nevertheless. Someone must rule, Ms. Leblanc, someone must decide, since others don't, won't. And let's confess it, there are those impossible gifts that cannot ever be given. Let the sobbing commence. Under bedspreads, behind bitty knuckled fists, let the sobbing commence. No matter, those gifts will not arrive.

There's just one sufferable mantle to wear when you're The Emperor of No. I dare not let it slip off again. My own faithful punishment is my only escape.

*

Dear Ms. Leblanc:

What a kind (if puzzling) letter. Mistaken identity, don't you suppose, or another of those ubiquitous impostors of mine. Best wishes in locating the mysterious and lucky gent. I'm flattered, and please enjoy this absolutely unspilled bottle of Chardonnay.

*

Dear Myra:

I can't help with diseases. My deepest regrets, if you heard otherwise.

Love Is As Love Does!

E arning my bread in the creative writing business, obviously I do recognize how written words can wonderfully elucidate the story of love. Literary anthologies are chock-a-block full of geniuses doing just that. "For weal or woe I will not flee/ To love that heart that loveth me." Some clever soul was singing those lyrics before the year 1500, for pity's sake.

The pages I bring with me here today are much more humble and only date back to last April.

Straightaway let me 'fess up to being the "wise professor" mentioned in the young lady's class assignment that follows. And I believe I never ever copied and kept a piece of student work before, and certainly have never before shown a copy to my wife and asked for her critique. The motive with my wife I won't go into, except to comment that our marriage has gotten more interesting since the evening she accepted my request, or I'll call it "interesting" to avoid any unwanted private distractions. The grade I did eventually award this student— well, it was generous, very generous from numerous critical or technical standpoints, her outline format clearly marred by clumsy organizational leaps or sometimes lack of leaps, marred also by childlike simplicities, including those excessive exclamation marks. So whether I was "wise" or not I myself can't judge. BUT an autobiographical spark flickers through this mechanical outline which somehow, somewhere along the way, ignites and propels the student to a level beyond her actual mediocre abilities. As my wife blurted out, "This crazy outline thing is maybe really a poem, isn't it?" (Even though married to a creative writing instructor my wife factually hasn't read, to the end, more than thirty poems in her entire life. Don't ask me why.) Still I see the perception of her point. And oddly enough—speaking of crazy—this little sample of student handiwork I pick up again and again, at least once or twice every month. Every month!!

Creative Writing 200

<u>Assignment</u>: Outline for short story (could be a novel!)

Focus: Story about woman rediscovering her "life" at age 42

Focus: Effect of such a momentous rediscovery on protagonist/family/friends

Focus: Meanings (insights) learned from this experience by characters (hence also the reader!)

I. The Protagonist

    A. Description: 42 years young, 5'4", shapely 38-28-34, yesteryear hair style with frosted tips, cinnamon-hue eyes, face dominated by long but straight nose

    B. Background: daughter of poor pensioned soldier, sewed own dresses, worked summers, could not attend college due to money problems, married at 19, had children at 20 and 22, housewife as career

    C. Personality

        1. excellent household manager with spotless home—the Queen of the Vacuum Cleaner type

        2. keen on following family's financial gains—"You kids'll

have your chance at college."
3. loves her two children
   a. always a birthday
      party
   b. always a good "nurse"
      during sicknesses
   c. always a sympathetic
      ear
4. not vain, but proud of her
   figure, 2nd runner-up as high-
   school homecoming queen—
   believes she didn't win
   because her nose wasn't small
   enough and because her family
   wore hand-me-down clothes

II. Other important characters

A. The husband: 4 years older than wife,
steady white-collar worker,
thinning hair, tender smile, hobby
of playing (sometimes squealing)
the clarinet

B. The son: age 22, B.A. in engineering,
recently employed in Atlanta,
recently engaged to school
girlfriend

C. The daughter: age 20, college junior
but still not altogether sure "what

she wants to be" and struggling
"just a bit" academically
D. The brother-in-law: the husband's
younger brother, formerly a
financial adviser who last year (he
claims) made $420,000 from an
industrial park
E. The neighbors: Mr. & Mrs., have lived
in next-door house for 18 years and
are like honorary uncle & aunt to
the children
III. Dominant image or controlling
metaphor
A. Change (external) images
1. seasonal changes
a. falling leaves, changing
colors
b. cooler days, nippy nights
c. people dressing differently
(coats, scarves, etc.)
and <u>appearing</u> different
2. generational changes
a. husband's father died 7
months ago
b. son away from home and
about to be married
(woman shown emotionally

reading his letters)

    c. daughter away at school
(woman shown emotionally
reading her letters)

    d. neighbors' children grown
(quiet yards)

    e. quiet (lonely?) household

B. Change (interior) images

    1. paperback "romances" found on
woman's nightstand

    2. she begins watching noontime TV
"soap operas"

    3. she is seen examining face and
figure in mirror

IV. Conflict

A. Woman announces she has fallen in
love with brother-in-law

B. Will woman divorce husband?

C. How will family react?

V. Exposition

A. Woman tells husband

    1. in bed at night says "I have
something unusual to tell
you."

    2. or, over phone says "Can you
come home early? Marky and I
want to talk to you."

    3. or, at dinner, passing the
       potatoes, says "You know how
       much I'd hate to hurt you."

    4. or, during their Sunday brunch,
       eating their weekly French
       toast, says "You know how much
       I appreciate what you've done,
       over the years, for the kids
       and me."

B. Woman tells son

    1. writes, "I never thought I'd be
       writing such a letter."

    2. says, "You recall how I've
       always admired your uncle
       Mark?"

C. Woman tells daughter

    1. writes, "I never thought I'd be
       writing such a letter."

    2. says, "You being a young woman
       now and being interested in
       the arts, you know that
       feelings sometimes take
       strange turns."

D. Woman tells neighbors

    1. says to Mrs. neighbor, "Love
       takes strange turns."

    2. says to Mr. neighbor, "I want us

all to stay friends."
E. Woman tells everyone
    1. that she and brother-in-law are
       ideally suited
       a. have similar tastes
          i. travel
          ii. dancing
          iii. "romantic" things
       b. brother-in-law wants to
          spend his money on
          adventures for the two
          of them
       c. brother-in-law has
          learned lessons from
          failure of two previous
          marriages
       d. woman has learned
          lessons from a marriage
          of "convenience"
       e. they want a chance for
          fuller happiness and not
          be "two ships passing in
          the night"
    2. her family will be less affected
       now
       a. the children are reared
          and independent

      b. husband can have his
         widowed mother move in
         and do household chores
         and cooking
    3. time at last for woman to lead
      her own life

VII. Climax

  A. Christmas Eve dinner at home

    1. description: Christmas tree with
      the old familiar family
      ornaments and a pile of
      colorful presents underneath,
      candles on the mantle, glowing
      log in the fireplace, advent
      calendar on the wall, dust
      covers off the sofa and
      upholstered chairs, dinner
      table with extra leaves set
      for 9

    2. ALL persons are in attendance

      a. the woman

          i. wearing a dressy linen
            pantsuit and pearls

         ii. chattering at speedy
            rate

        iii. many quick trips to
            kitchen and back

b. the husband

    i. wearing his 23-year-
old wedding suit
(plenty wrinkled)
which he has dug out
of the attic

    ii. not saying much

    iii. sitting beside his
wife in usual spot

c. the brother-in-law

    i. wearing bow tie and
smoking pipe

    ii. smiles, full-voiced
responses

    iii. sitting at other
side of the woman

d. the husband's mother

    i. happy in the kitchen,
happy at the table

    ii. catches up on the
news from her
grandchildren about
Atlanta and
about college

    iii. obviously has not
yet heard the "big"
news from her own

```
             two boys
  e. the son
       i. looking rather rumpled
          and unshaven
      ii. tight-lipped, except
          to his fiancée and
          grandmother
  f. the daughter
       i. did not sleep the
          night before
      ii. has distractedly
          misbuttoned her
          pink-and-cream dress
          which she has just
          decided is a silly
          dress anyway
     iii. has absolutely no
          appetite
      iv. in fact, feels ill to
          her stomach
  g. the fiancée
       i. only her 3rd visit
          ever to future
          husband's home
      ii. pale-faced, in a pale
          yellow tube dress
          with short sleeves
```

        iii. her paleness (yet
           roving eye)
           indicates that she
           has been given the
           shocking report
           about her future
           mom-in-law
   h. the neighbors
      i. paired together at
         table's end
      ii. Mr. neighbor talks
         loudly in
         indiscriminate
         directions
     iii. Mrs. neighbor takes
         many sips of water
B. Instigating act
  1. the husband comments, "This is
     my wedding suit, Mom."
  2. the husband's mother, "Truly?
     Hear that everyone?"
  3. the woman, "Remember when those
     lapels were in fashion?"
  4. the husband, "I love her now as
     much as then. More."
  5. the husband's mother, "Oh, how
     sweet. How lucky you are,

  Arlene dear."
6. the brother-in-law, "We all
  still love her, Mom."
7. the neighbors
  a. Mrs. neighbor spills her
   water
  b. Mr. neighbor, "Hey there,
   skinny, it fits you even
   today, by golly."
8. the husband's mother, "Well, of
  course we all love her."
9. the husband
  a. silent for a time, as food
   is served
  b. speaks, to his mother, to
   his wife
   i. "But does she still
    love _me_?"
   ii. "Did she ever love
    me?"
C. Rising action
 1. the husband's mother surveys the
  table
  a. she seems to show her age
  b. various memories of her
   husband pass through
   her mind

      c. says, "What on earth," etc.
2. the woman slumps, signifying
    that now Christmas Eve dinner
    has been spoiled
      a. has some cooling
         trepidations
      b. looks to brother-in-law for
         support
3. the brother-in-law explains
      a. apologizes for disrupting
         everybody's meal, and
         their lives
      b. he's smooth
      c. tells his mother that he
         and brother's wife have
         "found" each other
4. exchange between brother-in-law
    and his mother
      a. his mother, "What on
         earth," etc.
      b. brother-in-law, "We fell in
         love."
      c. his mother, "You and
         Arlene?"
      d. brother-in-law, "Yes,
         ma'am."
      e. his mother, "You and your

brother's wife?"

    f. brother-in-law, "That's
right."

    g. his mother, "After 23 years
suddenly you and Arlene?"

    h. etc.

5. the mother would like to hear
"What happens next?"

    a. the woman, "We don't know
exactly."

    b. the husband, "I love her."

      i. wants her here

     ii. wants the family
together

    c. the brother-in-law, "We
intend to be a couple."

    d. the mother, "Do you mean
married?"

      i. sees mental pictures
of her two little
boys at play, back
as children

     ii. sends mental cries of
distress to the dead
father of the boys

    e. the brother-in-law, "We
intend to become a

married couple."

    f. the son says something explosive to his uncle

        i. "Go marry one of your old wives again if you need to marry somebody."

        ii. or, "You haul your butt out of here and keep it away."

    g. the fiancée gasps

    h. the neighbors, "Should we excuse ourselves?"

    i. the daughter, "Dinner's getting cold."

D. Concluding action

    1. brother accuses brother

        a. "What kind of thievery is brother stealing from brother?"

            i. always took care of younger brother (gives examples)

            ii. never did harm to younger brother's wives

            iii. Thou Shalt Not Covet

   Thy Neighbor's Wife

 b. Mrs. neighbor blushes

 c. brother-in-law responds,
   "Did not steal your
   wife!"

   i. pounds table, yanks at
    bow tie, etc.

   ii. falling in love is
    not stealing or
    unfair (all's fair
    in love and war)

   iii. their relationship
    has been open and
    "above board"—ask
    "anyone," etc.

2. the neighbors dispute certain
 inaccuracies

 a. Mr. neighbor clears his
   throat, mumbles about a
   tan Mercedes arriving
   next door in the early
   afternoons and blinds
   being drawn, other odd
   signs

 b. Mrs. neighbor kicks Mr.
   neighbor under the table

 c. many around table construct

       imaginary (?) scenes

       i. secret meetings, with
           glances over the
           shoulder, whispered
           messages, nervous
           watching of the
           clock

      ii. passionate meetings,
           rushing to one
           another's arms,
           possibly in this
           very dining room,
           "O, Marky!"
           "O, Arlene!"
           "We shouldn't!"
           "We must!"

     iii. lurid meetings, with
           piles of underwear,
           with jiggly flesh, a
           frenzy of forbidden
           fruit

3. the nephew accuses his uncle

  a. compares the situation to
     <u>Days of Our Lives</u> script

     i. his uncle is the
        philanderer

    ii. his mother is the

        innocent prey
  b. remarks on his uncle's
     "money talk and other
     bull manure claims"
4. the uncle scolds his nephew
  a. "Should have your mouth
     washed out."
  b. "Should have a spanking."
5. the nephew warns his uncle to
   "stay away" from the woman
6. the uncle warns his nephew
  a. (making a comparison) "I'll
     stay away from Arlene
     when you stay away from
     your girl there in
     yellow."
  b. (sarcastically) "Unless
     you're getting cold feet
     and would just as soon
     dump the southern belle."
7. the finacée sputters, etc.
8. the nephew says, "I'll dump
   something all right," and
   dumps the bowl of salad greens
   into his uncle's lap
9. the woman's mother-in-law moans,
   etc.

10. the woman questions her own
    self
    a. cleans up salad, patting
       brother-in-law gently
       with napkin
    b. asks herself out loud, "Am
       I selfish to want a
       second chance?"
    c. asks herself, "Am I wrong
       to think about becoming
       somebody besides the same
       wife and same mother?"
    d. asks herself, "Is it wrong
       to think I'm not old and
       finished yet?"
11. the husband repeats his wife's
    name several times
12. the brother-in-law departs,
    pretty much defiant
    a. coolly lights his pipe,
       straightens cuffs, etc.
    b. leaves a statement behind
       at the door
       i. (to the woman)
          "Certain people can
          never be apart,
          even when they

             separate for a few
             hours."
          ii. or, "Arlene will
              settle this when she
              follows her heart."
    13. the daughter also retreats,
       fearful she may vomit up the
       Xmas dinner she never ate
VII. Recapitulation of conflict
  A. The week after the dinner party
    1. the son and fiancée back in
       Atlanta
    2. the woman's mother-in-law has
       also left
    3. the neighbors off visiting their
       own children
    4. the daughter at home for
        remainder of school holiday
    5. the husband not saying much
    6. the woman saying a lot
  B. The family house fills with tensions
    and shadowy fates (setting)
    1. describe hollow rooms
    2. describe ominous atmosphere
  C. The father and daughter
    1. smiling wanly, he asks her, "You
       anyhow won't ever quit being

    my daughter, will you?"
2. she answers, "No, I won't."
3. she silently wishes he would
   stand up and fight to hold on
   to his wife
   a. watches him poke at his
      food, watches him in the
      evenings sitting, staring
      nowhere, with a slipper
      dangling from the toes
      of one foot
   b. tries to imagine father and
      woman together on
      daughter's birthday, 20
      years ago, and on her
      conception day, 9 months
      before that
D. The woman and daughter
   1. mother-daughter camaraderie
      a. woman says, "At least _you_
         understand me," putting
         arm around daughter,
         etc.
      b. daughter considers that
         perhaps she does
         understand
         i. life wants to trap

everybody on the
worn paths of
expectations
    ii. maybe her mother is a
rare brave one, a
heroine
  2. the woman confides that she will
make her decision before
daughter returns to college
E. The uncle (brother-in-law) and niece
(daughter)
  1. have several extended talks
together
  2. he says, "Sure glad you're on
our side."
    a. gives her a bunch of
affectionate squeezes,
etc.
    b. she realizes he is
accidentally caressing
her breasts under her
sweater
F. The woman and daughter
  1. daughter tries persuading mother
to forget the brother-in-law
    a. cites 9 or 10 good reasons
to abandon him

      b. can't quite bring herself
         to add the 11th and best
         reason: he's a rat
  2. when daughter finally leaves for
     school the woman hands her a
     sealed envelope
  3. on return trip the daughter
     opens envelope and reads the
     message inside
      a. "I will be going to live
         with your uncle Marky."
      b. "Please support me on
         this," etc.

VIII. Denouement
  A. Daughter back on campus
    1. feels that her world is flying
       into pieces
    2. weeps in her dorm room at nights
    3. desperately searches for way to
       save the outcome
      a. turns creative writing
         class assignment into her
         family's story
         i. scenes of happy family
            past
         ii. scenes of Xmas Eve
            dinner fiasco

iii. scenes of family's
broken hearts
iv. scene of brother-in-
law propositioning
Mrs. neighbor
(successfully?)
v. curtain falls on total
domestic tragedy
b. daughter types up story
outline and submits it
to wise college professor
i. assignment receives B+
grade
ii. proud daughter mails
class paper to
mother "just to brag
how well school's
going"
4. the woman reads her daughter's
detailed outline
a. "light bulb" clicks on
b. woman see foolishness of
turning brother-in-law
into love object
c. but is it too late?
5. woman returns to own home
a. scene of woman and husband

        meeting at front door

          i. wordless

          ii. eyes moist

    b. scene of woman and husband

        sitting on sofa

          i. wordless

          ii. palms press together

             (equals 4 palms)

6. words of regret and words of joy

    finally shared by almost all

    a. mother-in-law writes brief

        note, "Somebody is

        smiling in his grave

        right now."

    b. son and fiancée have super

        wedding

          i. Mr. & Mrs. neighbor

             sit in front row at

             church

          ii. brother-in-law uncle

             sits in the last row

7. happy ending

    a. woman and husband sail off

        on 5-week world cruise

        (thanks to their 401k

        savings credit)

    b. thanks to their daughter

IX. Theme

    A. Love Is As Love Does!

    B. Get good grades in school??? (Joke!!)

The Strange Science of Estrella

Perhaps I'm an audacious eighteen. Perhaps I'm eighty, and wise, and tired. Either way you may hardly care. But dear observer, dear person out there, that is my sole purpose—making you care. By shifting the gravitational force of your attention even slightly in my direction you add a weight to my life. I need you. I need advice. The world is big and I feel small. All confessionals, no doubt, are a form of begging.

I first saw Estrella at a distance, yet that distance never prevented her silvery eyes from hurting me. They did. How beautiful was she? What a pointless question. Although still a stranger to me, I was angry with her, instantly, for making me helpless.

Am I eighty? Because the thought of her makes me weary, if not wise. Or am I eighteen? Because Estrella I love you with the constant ecstatic stupor of first love.

While many might agree that consciousness is the major miracle of the cosmos, a better idea is, that intellect and emotion form their own cosmos.

*****

For unfathomable reasons she frightened me and I avoided her for a full year. Maybe it was for two full months. Maybe for two eternal days, it was.

Finally I put myself into a cavernous room with her, at evening, with numbers of others standing around us, for safety. Except there was no escape. This unknown Estrella stood there illuminated under a brilliant light, or at least there was a brilliance coming from somewhere. She wore a soft sweater, joltingly sapphire, the color repeating itself with a further shock in her eyes. I needed to discover more. I was the moth drawn to a sapphire flame, approaching, approaching, closer, foolishly.

What was this creature? In my mind I used that word, that deliberate unpleasant word, since I had never before seen a person, woman or man, form so unique a picture. Bluntly judged, her features were but properly symmetrical, her body but predictably female, all pleasing enough, all familiar enough. Yet the rest of her. And I can't even quite explain what "the rest of her" might mean. Estrella struck me as some fabulous mongrel animal, where parts of different breeds come together, unexpectedly, in a magical way. Or more sensibly, she was like one of those genetic hybrids who occasionally get photographed on the Laplander steppes—north of the Arctic

Circle—where transiting outsiders had left behind their exotic ejaculate, creating the sole woman in her tribe with blonde hair or the only green eyes among the sable.

Now there stood Estrella before me. With those silver Nordic eyes. With her explosion of uncontrollable pitch-black curls, as much African as anything. With her flawless skin that duplicated pale Japanese porcelain. And there I stood, directly in front of her, tongue-tied, while my thoughts tumbled out of control among embarrassing questions. Would the back of her neck smell like flowers from a foreign country? Were her pubic tendrils still another wildly unexpected color—scarlet possibly? Did her areolas glitter golden, imitating a stripper's cliched pasties? Crazy, crazy notions, but I refuse to lie about them to you.

Was Estrella too strange, too different, and only I considered her beautiful? A friend would later tell me, "She's the handsomest plain woman you could ever hope to come across." I think that was his puzzled way to agree with me.

On that first night Estrella had eventually asked, out of simple curiosity, not smiling, "Are you staring at me?"

*****

Estrella didn't resist letting our lives overlap—initially for an hour or two, here and there. We met again, then again, then with regularity, in a routine that appeared to have very little to do with . . . what's the term . . . dating. Our first six times sitting together she ended up asking a version of "Are you staring at me?"

On the seventh time, preemptively, I said, "I'll be staring at you today."

She had to smile, and that damn smile made me dizzy with longing and loneliness. I wanted to marry her smile. Luckily—I suppose—in the beginning she smiled seldom, or otherwise sleep would have been short for me, lying in bed remembering the shine on her lips.

Marriage, did I say? That social construct seemed to belong from a lost culture.

When I once led Estrella to a chair in a restaurant, and kept her hand in mine, she turned a whiter shade of her paleness, which startled me into making a quick apology. She shook her head, and by way of apologizing herself, explained that no one else had ever held her hand romantically before. This announcement came from a woman old enough to have voted already in two American presidential elections.

I retain photographic detail of my menu from that lunch, after these many years, or from last year, or whenever. Served to me was a pretty BLT sandwich: toasted wheat bread cut into two exact squares by trimming off the crust, each square held by a wooden skewer with a bold yellow tassel. Also on my plate waited a vanilla scoop of cottage cheese topped with a slice of peach, quarter-moon shape, likewise bold yellow.

Probably I ate the food. But the only appetite I had was my curiosity—my insatiable and silent questions. What virgin object had fallen into my local patch of the planet from the outer space of innocence? Was Estrella, not realizing it, confessing that those lips were untouched by any man's, or even any nervous, fumbling boy's lips? Irresistible Estrella? Impossible.

"Go ahead," I said to her, "ask me if I'm staring."

*****

The day did come when I found out about the kissing. That memorable day was a literal daytime, an afternoon, as we sat on an invitingly obscure wooden bench, in an invitingly deserted neighborhood park.

There in the sunshine I heard my voice speaking. "I'd like to kiss you. I would." This seemingly is how an eighteen-year-old can dare to talk.

Estrella moved herself into me.

I asked, "Have you ever kissed a man before?" This seemingly is what an eighty-year-old could not resist from knowing.

"Never."

"Never. But why?"

She clearly did not find the fact unusual, and explained, as you might to a child, "Because there wasn't any *you* before, I guess."

This left me only able to say, "Does that mean then I should?" Seemingly this is how an idiot responds.

And our kiss. Please don't make me try to describe it. Well, it was the act that turned me into eighteen forever.

*****

There followed other days and also other nights and a share

of other kisses. And each separate kiss was as original as the first one, back when we sat there on that park bench, in that sunshine. Of course, I agree such claims are asinine, other than to us eighteen-year-olds. On the other hand, be advised that eighty-year-olds lack the energy to squander on deceptions, and lack the spirit to write fake romance.

I did experience a history about Estrella. It might have been a fevered vision, during a 102-degree temperature I suffered one whole dizzy weekend. Maybe it was a plain dream or maybe a lost memory that resurfaced. Or you guess.

In this history I visit her parents, who live in a parsonage, where the father is a vice-vicar in semi-retirement. Familiar with my name they happily accept my suggestion for a get-acquainted meeting, between the three of us.

The parsonage proves to be a traditional brick building decorated with the traditional climbing ivy. Inside, the rooms are spotlessly clean, the furniture all the more comfortable from the worn feel of much invited use. I sink into a cushy brown chair, thinking, with a shiver, "Estrella sat in this very chair as a child."

The mother has prepared an American version of what the British call "afternoon tea." Fancy crackers. Three cheese types, sliced, arranged on a circular china platter. A glass bowl with cantaloupe wedges. Three doughnut types, halved, sloping up the sides of a wicker basket. A carafe of orange juice. A small pitcher of chilled water.

Fussing about among the food choices I do my best to

steal helpful snapshots of these parents. "That's one of my favorite cheeses," I tell the mother, looking her directly in the eye. Her eyes, a faded gray, only remind me of my own mother's eyes, or any mother's eyes. Indeed, she's a perfect plumpish representation of thoughtful motherhood, a treasured stereotype, born in Oklahoma to "native Okie stock," she informs me.

I take a bite of cantaloupe, a sip of orange juice. "Estrella is a brilliant woman," I offer, as bait.

"Now, sir, I can't take any credit for that," says the mother, modestly, but with conviction.

"Me neither," adds the father. Both parents speak mildly, to the point of blandness, in the most positive sense of that abused term. The father, thoroughly and professionally committed to being polite, is a slim fellow not much taller than the mother, with dusky complexion and lank black hair. His own father immigrated from New Delhi as a youngster.

"Don't be modest," I probe, taking another melon wedge.

"No, no," says the father, "we don't take much credit of any sort for Estrella. She's Estrella. We learned that lesson long ago."

"You can take credit for her hair color at least."

"Not even that. Because of the adoption, you see."

The mother echoes, "Because of the adoption."

With the melon between my teeth, I myself repeat, messily, "Because of the adoption."

The father says, "There must be a black-haired someone

back there someplace, but we'll never know who."

I put my melon wedge down on my plate with the tooth marks showing.

"Never," says the mother.

I pick the melon wedge up again, completing my bite, giving me a mouthful to chew before I patch together any sentence. "So the agency, the adoption agency, wouldn't release personal information. Because of restrictions. Legal restrictions."

"Not that at all," says the father. "They had no record of this baby."

The mother says, "She was only a week old. That was everybody's guess, anyway. Try a doughnut?"

I do. A coconut half and a glazed half. "But at the hospital?"

The father says, "No records at any of the hospitals."

I eat the doughnuts, both halves, quickly. "I'm stumped."

The father says, "It's rare, even for foundlings."

The mother says, "Even for foundlings."

I nod, as if I know what the bejeebers they're talking about. "Does that happen anymore, nowadays? A foundling?"

They both assure me that, oh indeedy, it can happen, and that it did for them, a sleeping baby in a cardboard box, left right there in front of the parsonage door that I had just opened. I start again with another cracker-and-cheese sandwich, another cantaloupe wedge, and another doughnut half. The mother beams appreciatively at my hunger. I wonder aloud, "How is it possible then. The procedure. A baby from nowhere. On your doorstep. Becoming your child."

With a slap on his knee and a tiny groan, the father says, "A mountain of paperwork, a Mount Everest of paperwork, is how it works. First the baby has to become a legal thing, and second, you have to become its legal parents, and third, and seventh, and so on."

The mother says, "A mountain of red tape. Fortunately, we were ideal candidates for adopting. And we always used to joke, 'Finders-keepers-losers-weepers' is the rule. But the truth is we had no children—couldn't have any—and she was a gift to us from above." She points heavenward.

The father says, "People laugh when we tell them why we named her Estrella, and why we call her a handful of stardust that drifted down from way up above, and that read the WELCOME doormat at our front door."

The melon bowl is empty, the cheese slices down to three. The mother intends to resupply the table, but I rise for my goodbyes, saying, "Estrella is a wonderful mystery."

That remark prompts the father's recollection. "When she was twelve . . . about twelve . . . we talked ourselves into submitting a sample of her saliva to one of those commercial DNA companies, one of those businesses, you know, who do your genetics, your background, and advise about your family genealogy. We waited, and about every two months the company would send us another kit, claiming we had contaminated the sample somehow, because their lab could make no sense of it. I believe we tried . . . just how many kits was it?"

"Four, I believe," answers the mother.

Leaving I make sure to give them both a lengthy hug.

*****

Every hour of every decade a foundling stays a fresh discovery to find, which translates to mean that you never truly discover the foundling. And this was Estrella's glory to me.

I would, on many more than one occasion, use my hand, or perhaps use a single finger to better concentrate focus, and follow the dark corona of her hair spread against the cream of a bedroom pillow, and follow the dark wings of those arcing eyebrows that she never bothered to shape, and drop down to sweep gently across her curiously elongated eyelashes, closing them, and stroke across the sculpture of her cheekbones and down to touch her lips, where I would usually pause to explore with a kiss.

"I love to study you," I would explain to her.

She would smile in return.

"I love your perfection."

Smiles. To my good fortune Estrella had come, dependably, to treating me with showers of smiles, often in place of speech.

"That is, your perfection for me."

Smiles.

"I love how you surprise me."

Smiles. Her patience with me was boundless.

"That is, you surprise me by never surprising me."

She would touch my face back, smiling.

"You have a perfection of no surprises."

A smile. A touch.

"I love loving you."

*****

The hour arrived, the year arrived, whichever, to undress Estrella. We had kissed. We knew. We knew without any talk.

Estrella lay atop my bed, like a bride on a nuptial bower. She even wore a white dress, a loose summer dress belted at the waist by the lavender accent of a sash, her sandals already off, her face already flush. And she was smiling her smile.

I did pull the lavender sash. I did remove it and put the cottony piece against my cheek. All the while I continued to stare at Estrella, as I always stare at my Estrella. Under that thin dress I could see her breasts moving by her deepened in-and-out-and-in breathing. The sharp nook between her waist and womanly hips seemed ready for a man's grip, my grip, my clench. I swear, her bare toes by themselves were sensuous and exquisite enough to wrack my heart. Go ahead and snicker at my faintheaded prose.

The fact is, she was beautiful to the point that I had to fight back teariness.

I told Estrella, "I'm a little boy who has a birthday present on a table in front of him. He knows there must be a special something inside. But the gift is such a wonderful gift of giving, the best present he has ever seen—ever will see—that he doesn't want to open it, because then it will stop being a present. I must want my birthday to continue on into the next day and the next."

Estrella had said she understood, which she did, and joining me in retying her sash, Estrella most tenderly squeezed my arm, asking, "Stretch out here close for a nice nap? And you're not a little boy." She soon fell asleep. I used this as another opportunity to watch her, lucky me.

*****

I began to calculate methods for keeping Estrella safe from me. I dreaded that I would eventually open the gift, alter it, destroy Estrella's uniqueness. These fears began by eroding at the edges of my good sense. Next they ate toward the center of actual sanity, another danger to Estrella.

We might observe, most of us, that sanity—or lack thereof—can be a tightrope wavering in the wind between reality and delusion. The difference between the two can become a meaningless divide, and sometimes an unwelcome one. On this tightrope I teetered for the painful duration of one intense delirious week. Or was it over one bruising month. Or throughout an entire blurry year.

A true madman would have considered murdering Estrella. According to that diseased logic her beauty would then be preserved in an amber of captured immortality. But I, with a lesser degree of madness, only considered murdering myself. Yes, suicide, and seriously considered, or theatrically. Far better to lock in a memory of perfection than to eliminate the perfection altogether. Following this choice I would die with peace on my face, ending my life inside a spectacular human supernova, with lots of light and heat.

Still, as I realized in due time, that due time when the eighty-year-old managed to rein in the eighteen-year-old, killing myself would take me away from a greater light and warmer heat.

Hand-in-hand these days, walking alone with Estrella, I tell her, "You don't flinch anymore when I hold your hand."

She smiles, of course. Agrees.

I say, "We've done it enough before."

She smiles. "Never *enough*."

That pleases me completely. I stare—oh yes, still stare—at the paralyzingly electric silver of Estrella's eyes. She is such a remarkable foundling. "But I have to stop kissing you."

"You do?"

"I must."

"And why?"

"Because of my wife. She wants me to stop."

Estrella smiles. "I don't believe you."

"I know what I know."

"However, you know wrong."

"So? Has she told you to kiss me back?"

Estrella smiles. "She has."

Estrella's smile unfailingly reminds me of how closely it resembles Phoebe's. Phoebe is another astronomical reference, is my wife of thirty years, and the mother of our three fine children. I say, "Your smile reminds me of someone else's."

"Phoebe's," says Estrella. "I've heard her insist on exactly that herself. A thousand times."

*****

Correct, my wife knows about The Other Woman. Moreover, oddly, and awkwardly, they've been friends for ages. I do my best not to mention Estrella often, over the years. Or over the weeks or the hours. Or whatever. I gain only limited success, since my wife Phoebe, of all people, will question me about Estrella—right out of the sapphire blue. And very personal questions she brings up, forcing me to confess how addictively I still love my foundling.

My wife especially presses to hear about Estrella at night, when we're settled into bed, side-by-side, lights out, waiting for sleep. In the blind quiet—her voice close by my ear—my wife will use Estrella's name.

Immediately not sleepy, immediately not tired, I'll whisper back, "Shouldn't I say farewell to her at last, let her go? Let her escape, like a star hiding in the daylight sky?"

"No, no," urges my wife, "I don't want you ever telling Estrella goodbye."

I never object, certainly not. Yet without a goodbye, what is fair or even safe for any of us, I ask the darkness around me, and ask you.

Twin Sisterhoodlums

(Act One, Scene One)

Scene: Twin sisters sit at a dining table, the meal finished, two bottles of wine in view, one bottle already two-thirds empty.

Sister #1 I'm thinking we should lay off the Merlot and concentrate on our decision. Let's put our minds right down to it.

Sister #2 I only had one more glass than you. I counted.

Sister #1 That wasn't a criticism of you, by the way.

Sister #2 Supposedly I'm the big drinker here.

Sister #1 You are.

Sister #2 What I mean is, I hold my liquor better. It takes more booze before I get buzzed.

Sister #1 That wasn't a criticism either, okay? I just figure we should set a damn wedding date so the whole world doesn't start to scratch its head. Or before Stevie

and Harold start to scratch their heads, especially,
or before they scratch their heads more than they
already scratch their heads.

Sister #2 Right, right, right. But no shit, I'll think clearer with
another glass of wine. That may sound crazy except
it's true.

Sister #1 *(With a dismissive wave of a hand.)* I'm your sister,
not your mother.

Sister #2 *(Pouring, drinking.)* Now then, Sis. A question
first. Is there, really, such a rush, really, about this
wedding date? Yeah, we need to get on with
everything, sure. But I feel like being in a race
here. I feel a bit short of breath.

Sister #1 *(Takes a deliberate sip from own wine glass. Stares
over at sister.)*

Sister #2 You're not kinda sorta short of breath yourself?

Sister #1 What we're short of is *time*. These engagements—
yours, mine—got announced fourteen months ago.
Wait . . . wait . . . make that fifteen months ago.

Sister #2 You sneaky calendar-watcher you.

Sister #1 We're turning into an EMBARRASSMENT.
Should I spell the word out?

Sister #2 Some embarrassment along the way is no excuse
to start sweating the calendar. Embarrassment we
can survive.

Sister #1 *(Another sip, another stare.)* Sweating is it. Do you
want me to talk about the calendar? Do you want

that, me talking about the calendar again?

Sister #2 Uh-oh. Is this the age thing?

Sister #1 It's the age thing.

Sister #2 Please not the age thing.

Sister #1 Too bad. 'Cause I'm talking about the age thing anyway.

Sister #2 Let me beat you to it. I'm 36. You're 36. There, that's the age thing.

Sister #1 Listen. Every week I pull out another gray hair.

Sister #2 I emptied out the bathroom wastebasket yesterday and saw 'em. The hair. I guess we haven't dumped our wastebasket in three months, by that one-a-week count.

Sister #1 Ha-ha. You're just lucky that Stevie likes blondes. You hide any gray hair that comes along.

Sister #2 I'm not a blonde.

Sister #1 Blonde-in-a-bottle then.

Sister #2 Is that another crack about too much wine? *(Takes an oversized defiant swallow.)*

Sister #1 *(Shakes head wearily.)* Bottle blonde then. Pardon me if that doesn't sound right either.

Sister #2 Besides, I only streak my hair.

Sister #1 *(Rapping knuckles on table top.)* Listen again. Listen to me closer. I want Harold. I want kids. I'm 36. You're 36.

Silence at the table.

Sister #2 You and Harold go have your kids.

Sister #1   Whatever are you babbling about? I intend to be married when I have children.

Sister #2   Exactly. Go off and marry Harold. He's a great catch—good-looking, likes to hug and be sweet, earns a ton of money. Go off and have your kids.

Sister #1   *(Rapping the table again.)* And that's just what we're yakking about, isn't it. And we've been yakking about this wedding for a year already, trying to plan the fricking day.

Sister #2   You do realize, it wouldn't have to be a joint wedding, after all, if that somehow doesn't work out, for any reason or other. We may be twins, but we "ain't identical twins," as Mom always lectured us. She never dressed us alike and she did our hair styles different and never let us date the same boy.

Sister #1   Well. I'm flabbergasted. I see you sitting over there and suddenly bringing up an entire brand-new idea, like maybe you forgot how we, and the guys, and our friends, and the whole world, have been talking about a double wedding.

Sister #2   The whole world again. It's rolling right at us. Look out, *jump*.

Sister #1   Calm down a minute. Okay. Let's both calm down and do a . . . review. We'll look back. Calm down and look back.

Sister #2   Calm. Got it.

Sister #1   And look back.

Sister #2   Looking back. Got it.

Sister #1   Think back to a February night last year, a rainy
night it was, when Harold and Stevie took us to
that dinner-date at Chez Chateau.

Sister #2   Never eat at a place where you can't quite
pronounce the name properly.

Sister #1   I wore my forest-green pantsuit.

Sister #2   The tight one that shows off your snazzy ass. Good
choice. Harold didn't have a chance.

Sister #1   You wore—

Sister #2   My tangerine off-the-shoulder summer dress. In
February. In the rain.

Sister #1   But which shows off the snazzy dècolletage of
your boobs. Stevie didn't have a chance.

Sister #2   Stop with the French. And I think the last time my
breasts were snazzy was about six Februarys ago.

Sister #1   I ate a salmon dish. And you ate, what?

Sister #2   I forget. No, I didn't forget. Also salmon, just like
you, dear sister.

Sister #1   The guys acted, I thought at the moment, on the
suspicious side, on the nervous side anyway, with
those sidelong glances and their forks bumping
against their plates.

Sister #2   And then came dessert.

Sister #1   Then came dessert. Crème brûlée.

Sister #2   Isn't that more French?

Sister #1   When dessert was served out came the fancy

jewelry boxes.

<u>Sister #2</u> Out came the tiny boxes.

<u>Sister #1</u> Both from Glitter City Jewels.

<u>Sister #2</u> Each one from Glitter City.

<u>Sister #1</u> Both a 1.25-carat solitary diamond.

<u>Sister #2</u> Both. Absolutely.

<u>Sister #1</u> Just imagine how these two clueless guys, clueless about jewelry, had to do the legwork to arrange the complete show, more-or-less rehearsing the steps, and do it for us, the twin sisters. Now everything flows together—in their minds—the proposals together, the wedding together. Hard to deny that it was plenty thoughtful of them to consider us like that—plenty touching, we can say.

<u>Sister #2</u> No argument. Very touching for a couple of guys, being that guys don't always jump straight into the emotional stuff with enthusiasm. Even their proposal declarations were touching, mainly because of the tongue stumbling that happened and keeping their voices low and out of earshot of the other diners. I wondered, afterward, if Harold and Stevie practiced their little speeches in front of each another, hoping to pick up feedback or tips for improvement. That'd be a hilarious scene to watch. "Harold, clue me in, how many times should I say 'I love you'? Would three times seem over the top?" "Certainly not, Stevie. Three is the minimum."

Sister #1   Honestly, I couldn't repeat whatever Harold said to me that night about marriage, other than the "Will you?" part.

Sister #2   Too busy eating your crème whatchacallit?

Sister #1   My head was too busy spinning to concentrate on anything, including dessert.

Sister #2   Well, Harold reached across and took your hand between his, both his, and cleared his throat, said, "My darling . . ." but his throat was choked up and he sounded like a fourteen-year-old instead of a forty-year-old. Then he pulled his hands back for his water glass, and took a big gulp. Then he held your hand again, with both of his again. "My darling" — I'm quoting now—"please tell me that we can put our two lives into one life. Please tell me that we will never separate, in spirit and body." I find that poetic and horny in the same sentence, don't you? "Please give me happiness forever." Finally he reaches the marriage question.

Sister #1   Wowee, some memory you have, my sweet. And not too shabby a proposal from Harold at that. I'll take it.

Sister #2   You did take it.

Sister #1   What about Stevie's? I can't recall his proposal either.

Sister #2   A proposal is a proposal, when a girl gets down to the bottom line. He followed Harold, and the second act on stage always needs to wave his arms harder to capture everyone's attention, sort of like being a second child, which he is, incidentally.

Sister #1   What a gentle soul. Stevie only needs a strong woman to give him a home and protect him inside those four walls. Some days I almost want to mother the fellow myself. For pity's sake, marry him and snuggle up together in front of a cozy fireplace in a cozy house. You're perfect for Stevie.

Sister #2   So you say. So Stevie says. Sometimes, like tonight, like right now, I ask myself if I need any man whatsoever. It's popular nowadays, you realize, women doing without men. Lots of talk about gender independence.

Sister #1   Watch me. I'm taking this bottle and filling up my glass, up to the top. *(Takes wine bottle, and with a dramatic flip of her elbow fills her goblet.)* Tonight —I see you and hear you—allowing yourself to run wild with your mouth. *(Tosses back a real swig of the wine.)* Tonight my sister announces she's been a secret lesbian all along. Whoops. Surprise.

Sister #2   My wild mouth didn't say lesbian.

Sister #1   Fine, because otherwise I can't figure out why you and Stevie always slip off and go away to your bedroom.

Sister #2   We don't slip away. We just thought you and Harold wouldn't wanna watch Stevie and me screw in the living room. And am I driving you to drink? You never pour yourself a second glass of wine at dinner.

Sister #1　*(Takes another long undainty swallow.)* Seems like you are. *(Squelches a modest belch.)* Driving me. To drink. Apparently you want the two of us to live here together, you and me alone, for a long long life of spinster joy. You cook on Monday, I cook on Tuesday, you cook on Wednesday, I cook on Thursday, and on and on, and so forth. I grocery shop on Saturdays, you do laundry on Sundays, and on and on, and so forth. I sing Happy Birthday to you on your birthday, you sing mine on my birthday. We decorate the Christmas tree together. On Christmas Day you play some carols on the piano while I pretend to sing them. Then you open my three presents to you and I open your three presents to me, although last Christmas you only gave me two.

　　Another silence intervenes at the dining table.

Sister #2　*(Refills her wine glass.)* You're awfully hard to shop for. I meant to find a third present, truly.

Sister #1　*(Sips. Twice.)* Sweetheart, are you afraid of being married, some kind of fear like that? Marriage is a giant change in our lives. Agreed. Are you anxious about it?

Sister #2　No.

Sister #1 Don't you like being in love even?

Sister #2 Yes.

Sister #1 There you go. See?

Sister #2 There I go. *(Drinks down half her glass.)*

Sister #1 Hold on. Why am I not believing you?

Sister #2 Don't ask dumb me why.

Sister #1 But I will ask you.

Sister #2 Have mercy, don't act the psychologist on me tonight. That's been your favorite teacher role ever since way back, when you got your period three months before I did.

Sister #1 Who understands you better than your twin sister, tell me. Nobody, that's who. Why don't you like being in love?

Sister #2 Are you repeating that silly question again? So I'll answer again. I like being in love. I *love* being in love.

Sister #1 I still don't buy it, somehow. I don't trust the look on your pretty face.

Sister #2 God above forgive me if I toss this glass of wine into my sister's pretty face instead of tossing it down my throat. *(Bolts down the last half of her wine.)* Like being in love? Hell yes. I want this man to run his fingers through my hair, want him to squeeze his fingers in my bottle-blonde hair, and I want to squeeze his hair back, too. Hell yes I want to snuggle up with him in front of that fireplace and giggle like a schoolgirl and gossip about the day and about our four children. Yes, hell yes, I love being in love. What's more, right now, tonight, I'm in love.

Sister #1 *(Sipping.)* Good, good. Now I believe you. I believe your face now.

Sister #2 Thank you.

Sister #1 Good, wonderful, how you love Stevie that much.

Sister #2 Well, yes.

Sister #1 *(Sipping.)* Well, yes.

Sister #2 Well, yes. Yes.

Sister #1 I'm curious. Does "well, yes" mean the same as your "hell, yes"?

Sister #2 Of course.

Sister #1 *(Shakes her head. Sips.)* No. No, it doesn't.

Sister #2 *(Shakes her own head).* You're impossible. I'm not going ahead with this conversation any longer. No siree.

Silence at the table.

Sister #1 You said you loved him.

Sister #2 Don't forget, I'm not a part of this conversation anymore.

Sister #1 I heard you just say "I'm in love."

Sister #2 Shhh. We're not talking about this, remember. So turn it off.

Sister #1 Mercy me—you've been lying. All along you've been lying. You're not in love and that's the problem, all along the problem. And quite a convincing liar you are. But finally I caught you.

Sister #2 Hey, my clever sister, you're wrong, very wrong. You didn't catch me in any lie.

Sister #1 I think I did. I see now, it's the logical explanation for the delay, the delays and delays, of the wedding.

Sister #2 I'm in love. And no lie.

Sister #1 Except I—

Sister #2 I'm in love. No except!

Silence at the table.

Sister #1 You're in love with Stevie. You want to marry Stevie.

Sister #2 This conversation really has ended.

Sister #1 Answer me, please, please. Please answer your sister. You want to marry Stevie?

Silence at the table.

Sister #2 *(Almost inaudible.)* No.

Sister #1 No.

Sister #2 *(Much louder.)* No.

Sister #1 *(Splashes another shot of wine into her glass.)* No wonder you wouldn't talk about this. I don't know how to talk about this myself. You love Stevie, but don't want to marry him.

Sister #2 *(Starts to refill her glass, instead stops, puts the wine bottle down again.)* You did catch me in one lie. You usually could spot my lies. Congratulations. I don't want to marry Stevie because I don't love Stevie.

Sister #1   Oh, my god.

Sister #2   Oh, my god.

Sister #1   Poor Stevie.

Sister #2   Poor Stevie. Poor Stevie, I suppose, though he would end up seeing through me and hating me then.

Sister #1   *(Sips. Sips.)* So you're *not* in love. And how convincing you were, with your oration, I have to admit.

Sister #2   Sometimes it's easy to lie.

Sister #1   When is it easy to lie to your sister?

Sister #2   When what's called a lie happens to be the truth.

Sister #1   The truth. What truth are we dealing with here?

Sister #2   The being-in-love truth.

Sister #1   *(Sips.)* You *are* in love.

Sister #2   I'm afraid so.

Sister #1   You're afraid. Why, why, are you afraid? And who the devil is this person? Do I know him, or his name at least?

Sister #2   I'll never never tell you. Put that notion out of your mind.

Sister #1   What the hell?

Sister #2   Never never. End.

Sister #1   You're pissing me off. You really are.

Sister #2   You shoved me into this discussion, this mess, and I won't go an inch further. End.

Sister #1   *(Shouting.)* You're pissing me off!

Sister #2 *(Shouting.)* Too bad!

Silence at the table.

Sister #1 *(Still seated, but noisily stacking some empty plates on her side of the table.)* I think those are . . . tears . . . starting up in your eyes.

Sister #2 No.

Sister #1 Yes.

Sister #2 No, I'm just mad.

Sister #1 You don't cry when you get mad. I know my sister.

Silence at the table.

Sister #1 And I can guess who the person is. From your endless protesting about the wedding, and the foot-dragging, I can guess, and no need for much guessing, either.

Sister #2 Please don't guess.

Sister #1 It's Harold. You love Harold.

Sister #2 Goddamn it. Please don't hate me.

Silence at the table.

Sister #2 Please don't hate me.

Sister #1 Be quiet.

Sister #2 I need you to forgive me.

Sister #1 Shut up. I'm thinking. *(Sips her wine.)* Did Harold ever give any signs back to you? Did he ever give you some encouragement . . . maybe touch you . . . make remarks?

Sister #2 Not really.

Sister #1 Don't you dare hit me with another one of those

cowardly "not really" answers. Did something happen?

Sister #2   But describing it will only turn everything into a huge production and it wasn't a huge production.

Sister #1   I'm waiting.

Sister #2   *(Looks briefly into her empty glass.)* Once Harold arrived first at our apartment, with you and Stevie still underway from somewhere. He gave me the usual "hello" peck on the cheek. Then sort of suddenly the peck slid over and his lips sort of fastened to the corner of my mouth.

Sister #1   What did you do next?

Sister #2   He surprised me, so I opened my mouth. In surprise. And I let my tongue move over to that same corner of my mouth. I don't know why. A reflex?

Sister #1   You know why.

Sister #2   Tonight I do.

Sister #1   Did you two ever talk about it after, or kiss a second kiss, anytime, anywhere?

Sister #2   No and no.

Sister #1   *(Rattling the dirty dishes, re-stacking them, with no actual purpose.)* Stevie will have to hear about all this, and the sooner the more humane.

Sister #2   Certainly. I'll tell him tomorrow.

Sister #1   Let me handle it with Stevie. Will you?

Sister #2   Let you tell Stevie?

Sister #1   I can picture your method. Your method is blurting it out like a bombshell, get it off your chest. But Stevie needs his hand held. Like I told you before, I do understand these super-sensitive types, always have. Remember high school?

Sister #2   Johnny Beyers?

Sister #1   Johnny Beyers. You remember.

Sister #2   I have to remember, after your all-night blabbering to me about how you lost your "semi-virginity." That was cute.

Sister #1   Johnny Beyers. Where is that darling redhead these days?

Sister #2   I feel guilty, I feel bad, with you talking to Stevie and Harold both.

Sister #1   I won't be talking to Harold. You will.

Sister #2   Explaining to him about the double wedding?

Sister #1   Explaining to him how you love him.

Sister #2   I can't. I can't. I won't.

Sister #1   You will.

Sister #2   It's too humiliating.

Sister #1   If you love him, you'll tell him. If you don't love him, you won't.

Sister #2   Jesus. But how.

Sister #1   Give him the other corner of your mouth to kiss. *(Smiles, wryly.)* See what that leads to, take it from there.

Sister #2   Meanwhile you and Stevie wait off somewhere, totally by yourselves, to discuss his sensitivity?

Sister #1   Who knows. Maybe Stevie'll grab my butt again and we can discuss that, the two of us.

Sister #2   What on earth?

Sister #1   A little accident that happened last summer.

Sister #2   What kind of grab was it? A serious one?

Sister #1   I'd classify it as a I-want-you-baby level of grab. But he misjudged me to be you. We were all at the July 4th party of Becca's, on her backyard patio, where that string of lights had half its bulbs out. It was practically pitch dark.

Sister #2   Sweetie, we don't look that much alike, you and me. And you're two inches taller than I am.

Sister #1   Well, anyway.

Sister #2   Were you wearing your green pantsuit?

Sister #1   Uh . . . I was.

Sister #2   FYI. I'll point out that Stevie, factually, has never grabbed my ass.

Sister #1   He never grabbed mine again either.

Both sisters rattle and stack dishes.

Sister #1   Your turn tonight to wash these dishes.

Sister #2   Maybe you think that Harold's the handsome one?

Sister #1   Not necessarily. But you do. That's the important issue.

Sister #2   Possibly.

Sister #1   Possibly you only want what it seems like you can't have.

Sister #2   Possibly.

Sister #1 I don't believe that for a single second.

Sister #2 Me neither.

More stacking of dishes.

Sister #2 In my mind I can't follow the path of where we go from here, or after tomorrow. It's fuzzy to me. Sorry.

Sister #1 We'll ask the guys if they want to switch for a while, a couple of months, you with Harold, me with Stevie. We'll say if they love us, they'll give it a try. If they don't love us, then goodbye, boys.

Sister #2 Holy Moly, I thought that I was supposed to be the weirdo comedian of the twin sisters.

Sister #1 Who's being funny? I'm not joking. They'll have to honor our sisterhood.

Sister #2 They might call us sisterhoodlums, or worse, for our using this blackmail, or whatever it is. Oh, brother.

Sister #1 Oh, sister.

Sister #2 Oh, sister.

Sister #1 We could have avoided trouble if you had said early in the game that you loved Harold, back before we got ourselves into hot water up to our necks.

Sister #2 I didn't because of another person I love very much.

Sister #1 Ah. What an excuse.

A few more dishes are idly moved about.

Sister #1 That last wine bottle is nearly gone and our glasses are empty, I see. Let's finish the sucker off. We deserve it and we need it.

<u>Sister #2</u> No, use the cork stopper. We don't need wine. Look here, that's the big drinker talking, you notice?

205

The twin sisters raise their empty wine glasses
for a wordless toast.

Geronimo from San Francisco

1.

What's in a name? asks a famous question. During those violent years of World War II his fellow soldiers called him "Geronimo from San Francisco," because they witnessed his secret wild solo raids against the German enemy in the North African night, and they had heard that his duffle bag might be full of severed German trophy ears. But he was not a renegade Chiricahua Apache and he killed, if he must, only out of love for a charming petite German girl. Her name—as he would explain to the Army psychiatrist— was Silke Wolke, who lived at 122 Adlersweg, Augsburg, Germany. In point of fact, he himself was not even from San Francisco, instead from Redwood City, which is nearby, close enough to ignore and not spoil a good rhyme.

His first nickname had been "GMC" for General Medals Corporation, an affectionate term since the soldiers pined for the Chevy, Buick or Oldsmobile built by General Motors Corporation that they drove at home not long ago, before 1942. This thumbs-up acronym was due to his quick rush of combat medals and promotion to sergeant. Yet after a time, when repeated mad bravery seemed more just ordinary madness, and after a time when the sergeant showed more appetite for dangerous deeds than for his food in the mess tent, to the uneasy soldiers the highly decorated sergeant became, in the end, a friendless Geronimo.

"This is *not* your *private* battlefield, Sergeant," an upset, or confused, officer once informed him, without raising his voice much. No one cared to threaten the sergeant directly. While this Geronimo without fail acted calm and civil, nevertheless here stood a man, at polite attention, said to slit throats by moonlight.

No surprise that eventually an order arrived for the sergeant to attend a mandatory evaluation session with Major Seymour Fiedelmann, M.D., an hour's bumpy ride rearward from the combat zone. The major held office in a large canvas tent with red medical crosses on its rooftop, and furnished inside, somehow, with genuine civilian wooden desk and chairs. Upon the desk rested several very fat file folders with the sergeant's serial number stenciled across the front. The two occupants in the privacy of the tent presented many contrasts: the major immaculate, slight, pallid, bespectacled, hunched forward in his seat, and standing there the sergeant, rangy, rough at the edges, his brown eyes and uncut brown hair blending with desert-browned skin. What the two had in equal measure was certainty of purpose. The little major felt no fear of Geronimo.

"Sit, Sergeant Lemay, sit. I read in here"—tapping the files on the desk—"that I could call you Sarge Starlight or Captain Midnight or how about The Grim Reaper. Have you heard the men using those names before?"

"Along with Kilroy Killed Here."

"That one missed making the reports. Otherwise I know your story quite well. Quite well." The major did know the story, *quite* well, and to prove it immediately began reciting the particulars of how a new soldier, private first class, arrived at the battle front, an interrogation/translator specialist in German, who had cooked up excuses to hitch rides with the HQ couriers collecting field reports from the company commanders, and while overnighting there had outright lied his way into tagging along with squads doing picket duty on the perimeters, and later with the sentinels perched at the edge of no-man's land, and finally he was wandering off by himself beyond where only snipers went. One thick dissolving dawn this Geronimo had surfaced, luckily with the correct American password, his Colt M1911 .45 pistol herding a pair of German sentries, their mouths stuffed full of sand to guarantee silence. The Army decided to award the private with his first promotion and first medal.

To create a legend or a scandal, a story repeats itself beyond reason. On many more nights the new corporal disappeared alone somewhere into the unnerving bareness of the Tunisian plains, helmet off, dabbed with his own home brew of camouflage paint, toting an extra (unauthorized) revolver and compact binoculars. Before darkness fell he always informed the closest lieutenant of his departure, without asking for permission, his tersely given logic more than once recorded in field notes as "The corporal stated that a family relative was an expert bowhunter who had taught him a big bag of stalking tricks." His subsequent rise in rank to sergeant and his recommendations for medals often had in their citations— too often had—such feeble nonsense as "Lost when seeking to find a latrine, the sergeant engaged the enemy, whereby he . . ." followed here by an enumeration of stolen German weapons, the precise location of German positions, and the occasional befuddled actual German soldier.

"No more citations can come your way," said Major Fiedelmann, "no more promotions. Do you understand *why*?"

"Yes, sir."

"Does that disappoint you?"

"No, sir."

"I thought not. Sit back, Sergeant, lean back and relax. Okay, I see that you *are* relaxed. Sergeant, you possess a high education, two university degrees, and I intend speaking directly, without any of the usual psychotherapy stratagems or maneuvers. You comprehend why we're together today.

You know already that your nightly adventures are abnormal, counter not only to military regulations, but a deadly threat to your own safety."

"Yes, sir."

"And so I need to determine why you do it, and if you intend continuing to do it. Please be honest with me. This is a difficult war and we can't waste time. All right. Let's jump straight in. Do you enjoy danger, Sergeant, or feel a craving or desire for intense excitement? To put it simpler, do you like being scared shitless? Is it—remember I said be frank—sexual for you in any sort of way? For example, do you ever masturbate when out there by yourself?"

"No on all counts, sir."

"No on all counts. All right. Let's go to the main issue then. Can you imagine changing your pattern, tomorrow or next week, changing your motives, whatever they might be, and stopping these strange outings of yours?"

"No, sir."

"All right. I asked for honesty, and I received it, which is appreciated. A lesser man would have lied his way out of this hole we're in here. All right. Sergeant, if I use the term 'freelance berserker' would you understand me?"

"I think so, sir."

"While it doesn't happen often in our army—rare in fact— we do have our case studies, where war is a fun party for homicidal deviates, a perhaps once-in-a-lifetime license to murder with free heavy weapons provided by our own USA.

And I look at you, Sergeant, and I ask myself, is that *you*? Are you a real Grim Reaper that your buddies talk about?"

"I probably don't have any buddies, sir."

"Are you a killer?"

"Sir, I can't answer."

Major Fiedelmann studied his oversized steel-rimmed wristwatch, oversized at least on his spindled wrist, using the protracted squint to shuffle his mental cards. "I have another appointment due," he informed himself and the sergeant, "plus I was scheduled to submit, today, my recommendation on whether or not to send you back homeside, to the States." But in no apparent hurry the major began thumbing the sheets inside those folders on his desk, not reading them, merely riffling the pages with a monotonous flip-flip-flip noise. "I noticed your academic honors," said the major, "and I noticed you refused the Army's request to attend Officer Candidate School, making a little stink over the issue."

"Yes, sir. I chose to be a shooting soldier right away at the front, sir."

"Your great wish to be a shooting soldier is the puzzle, is it not. And your assignment as translator has been a disappointment no doubt, although you found other solutions, shall we say. Tell me, Sergeant, do you have a special animosity against German people?"

"No, sir."

"Is your own family of German heritage?"

"Swiss and British more or less, sir."

"You have those two degrees—bachelor's, master's—in German language and literature from Stanford University. Your German is officially rated as *native speaker*."

"An academic specialty, sir."

"But *native speaker*?"

"I was a motivated student, sir," said the sergeant. "More specifically, I found myself in love with a German girl, a foreign student on campus."

"Sergeant?" The major removed his glasses, although the blinking soft focus of his eyes indicated that he could not see well without them.

"By graduation we were engaged, sir. At the moment, sir, she still lives in Germany."

"Hold the horses. Put on the brakes. Let me count to ten. Better, I need to count to a hundred. What the devil are you telling me? That you do your nighttime stage show in order to get to Germany? Faster? Because you . . . love a girl there?"

"Yes, sir."

Now the major did check his watch with a more practical intent. "All right. Waiting outside my tent is an eighteen-year-old infantryman from Tallahassee who shot himself in the foot, on purpose. Quite a different tale from yours, we might judge, except the boy was married shortly before sailing over here. All right. All right, all right, all right. I'll be requesting one more meeting with you before my decision. Please get out so my head can stop spinning."

"Yes, sir."

2.

A dusty wind slapped and scratched against the tent's walls, a miserable morning, identical to most mornings in this tortured land. Absent from Major Fiedelmann's desktop was the bother of any file folders and in their place steamed a mug of coffee, reeking its bitterness to the heavens. The major projected a figure ready for stern duty: clean-shaven, damp hair freshly combed, uniform pressed and exemplary. He stated the rules for their session. "Today, Sergeant, you will do the talking. You will elaborate about this lady, your fianceé. No more of these one- or two-word sentences from you. Sergeant, you will begin at the beginning and end only at the end. Sergeant, you will spill your guts out today."

The sergeant need not stretch far to retrieve the details for the major. No, the opposite of far. Of course he will deliver to Dr. Fiedelmann only a cautious protected monochrome version of his story, while the sergeant's own simultaneous memories blossom with a rainbow palette. Rainbow palette? To him there could be no possible hyperbole about Silke Wolke.

Even at the first, back at the absolute first, when she entered a crowded Stanford lecture hall, circled anxiously about, finally locating an empty seat next to his, even then everything he saw and felt about her registered at an outer limit. "Have I here the proper class of Mr. Professor Fitch?"

she asked, her English spiced with numerous sweet missteps and struggling to Americanize its British imitation. She waited for an answer, looking up, not a stroke of cosmetics on her face, nothing to distract him from the gray-with-green eyes or green-with-gray, whichever the ceiling lights chose to reflect at any instant. There was no mistaking her for an American girl. Her midnight-color hair swept forward along the sides into what people call a pixie cut, yet with sufficient length to touch her temples, resembling, in his agitated mind in those initial moments, a crown of feathered ebony. Trimly tailored black tweed slacks met up with strapped wooden sandals. And that burgundy sweater hugging her, expensive cashmere it was, and worth every cent. "The correct room," he reassured her, lacking the gumption to continue with "and I beg you to come back, to sit beside me every single day." As she did, Major Fiedelmann, as she certainly did.

Fräulein Wolke was nineteen when she walked into that classroom. By the end of their first week he had bought a German dictionary, to help her over the language potholes. By the end of their first year he had switched his study program to German. After three years of days and nights together he knew that she would be coming to sit by him for the rest of their lives. When he started his graduate work they rented adjacent studio apartments, preserving the appearance of propriety. Naturally that lone wall never separated them and they examined one another as much as they read their books. Once he stood behind her as she sat at a desk, reaching down with the fingers of each hand to press against each fluted side of her throat, telling her to read the Rilke poems aloud, and he felt with fingertips those sensuous German gutturals, those teased umlaut vowels, those lavish sibilants. "Go on," he would say, then and often, "keep speaking in German." She would laugh and consent with a mock groan, "So I'll never learn English, but anyhow my German is improving." When he told her that he intended to master her language, by this fingertip osmosis preferably, she reminded him, "Who should care. You're already the master of *me*."

With her delicate figure and features, her cheeks and lips rose-tinged without makeup, Silke could be misjudged as childlike. Beware, beware, because that slim body and that intellect both packed a potent wallop. And although her complexion, especially without clothes, shone nearly a China Doll alabaster, Silke was not some dolly plaything of accommodating emotions. Her full name, Silke Wolke—by combining faulty English spelling with correct German—can be translated as "silky cloud." He elucidated this linguistic magic, as they lay on a bed, by running his hand down her naked supple back, over the rise of a hip, down again along a *silky* thigh. Her skin was the color of a pearl cumulus *cloud* that appears in the sunlit sky on warm summer afternoons. He so described to her why she was by name a bilingual beauty, and she responded by twisting his nose, hard, and labeling him "a silly guy in love."

He agreed. "Not much to argue with there. Let's admit

though that my translation skills are a stairstep higher than yours, and I'm sticking by the truth of my rhetoric."

"And I love you for loving me that much. But you're still a goofy boy."

Together, in August of 1941, they visited the Wolke home in Augsburg, where her father is a successful banker of importance. The substantial house at 122 Adlersweg commanded a fine downslope view of the city. Her parents were courteous and respectful. Her only, and younger, brother turned out to be a male copy of his sister—slight and refined of build, a handsome kid, almost pretty, friendly as blazes to the American, an all-around excellent candidate for a brother-in-law. His name was Stefan and in an aside he whispered, "Mom and Dad had an affection for names beginning with *s*, no?" "Just consider," he had whispered back to Stefan, "since my name's *S*-pencer, we form a perfect trio." Soon—if not already—Stefan would be old enough to wear a military uniform, a troubling thought. But on these August 1941 days, as a family group, they enjoyed the late summer weather, ignored the war bulletins, went picnicking on the greens along the Lech River, wicker baskets heaped with fresh bakery goods.

On December 1, 1941, Silke made a return trip for the Christmas holidays in Germany. On December 7, 1941, as the radio in California reported the Japanese war attack in Hawaii, he forgot to breathe and wondered what this news meant for him. It meant the worst of possibilities. And it meant that this sergeant was now on the coastline of Tunisia, only the Mediterranean Sea away from Europe, in a hospital tent with a major who was about to send him back to America.

That major was peering down into his coffee mug, musing. "Well. All right. That has to be a compelling history of yours, because I forgot to drink this java juice." Slowly he raised his usual sloped shoulders upward into their authority position, the posture of a Major Seymour Fiedelmann, M.D. "All right. Let's settle up now. I admit to conditional sympathies with you. I can appreciate your compulsion to be in action, that is, to feel yourself in command of a destiny, putting yourself in *motion* toward an important goal. I do appreciate that. Yet I remind myself that I am the doctor and you are the patient, and you *are* a patient, Sergeant Lemay, howsoever much we may dislike that reference. Bluntly—as we must be now with each other—you are what we medically consider 'a danger to yourself.' In other words, Sergeant, if I don't send you home immediately, the Army will ship you back to California sooner or later in a box, likely sooner. Then you'll never meet up again with your fianceé, will you. Don't worry, don't worry, this won't be a Section Eight mental disability discharge, not with those medals and citations of yours. The report will recommend a simple honorable transfer to stateside duties. I only hope you respect and grant me my requirement to be a good doctor."

"Major, I ask another requirement of you."

"You do?"

"Yes, sir."

"A requirement for me?"

"I do, sir. I ask that you be a better Jew than you are a good doctor. Anyway for this single time, sir. From your silence I believe you want me to explain. I will, sir. To begin, I've read *Mein Kampf.* Twice. I read the German newspapers. I visited Germany. Major, let's please not pretend we two don't know what's up there. Major, you might sit behind your desk during this war and save my skin or you can allow this sick-headed sergeant to be a sword in your hand. I can't express it in any other words. If for my own selfishly foolish purpose I put myself in Germany three hours faster than otherwise would happen, then the Army arrives three hours earlier. Sorry, sir. We did agree on honesty, sir."

The major took a long reflexive suck of his coffee and spat it back into the mug. "Awful," he said, "cold and awful. Excuse the splatter." In a desk drawer he found a tissue and blotted his chin. "You're a crafty smart-ass fellow." The wadded tissue got sent like an angry bullet into a wastebasket. "Come back tomorrow, late. After five o'clock."

The third and final meeting with Major Fiedelmann was grim and swift. "Do not give me anything resembling a thank-you," instructed the major, "and that's an order. Do *not* put a smile of any type on your lips."

"Yes, sir."

"I know about a young combat officer, a West Pointer, just made captain, an ambitious guy who sticks his nose into the middle of the fight. He agrees to take you for a scout as your sole duty, day or night, no hassles, no interrogation work, *if* you promise a genuine commitment to stay alive."

"May I meet the captain tomorrow?"

"He's waiting for you outside with his jeep."

3.

The captain, Captain Donald Delaney from the Chicago shore, walked with the sergeant to the seclusion of his jeep, parked under a camouflage tarp. "Welcome to my personal garage," he indicated. The captain was youthful yet matured by a taut intensity, his body fidgeting from some habitual preoccupation or other, his blue eyes bright and sharp, his cropped blonde hair already receding. Settled with the sergeant into the jeep's front seats, he said without prelude, "Sure, Geronimo, I know what the men call you. And the brass suspect you have only one oar in the water. I looked over your medico dope sheet, the spiel about compulsion *this*, delusional *that*, destructive *whatever*."

"Destructive narcissism."

"A swell mouthful. Is it on the mark?"

"Maybe halfway, sir."

"So you're crazy, Sarge?"

"But only halfway, sir."

"Ahh." The captain rapped a thumb knuckle thoughtfully against his front teeth, viewing the sergeant impatiently.

"It's obvious that you're taller and bigger than I am. You're a goddamn tougher soldier. And you're older than I am and kinda better looking. I graduated 14th in my class at West Point, but you're smarter and more educated. If you *are* crazy, who the hell am I to figure that out, or care, and I don't. This is business between us, yes, Sarge? In awhile we'll sail for Sicily, move on to the Italian mainland, with lots and lots of business to handle, and you and I can do each other some good."

"I like our arrangement. Incidentally, sir, could you pick me up one of those new Winchester M2 auto carbines, that paratrooper's version with the folding skeleton stock, pistol grip, 30-round clip?"

"Incidentally?" The captain had to unloosen, letting out a positively boyish grin. "Oh, Sarge, you sound like a *winner*. Okay, incidentally I'll try. What I can't give you are recommendations for any medals or promotions, and that's goddamn unfair."

"I never wanted medals."

"I believe you. I believe that, without having a clue about what does make you tick."

"I'm in a real hurry to reach Germany, sir."

Captain Delaney brushed away the pesky inevitable Tunisian gnats. "Yeah, right. We want to get this goddamn war finished and over."

"Let me lay it all on the table. My fianceé is waiting for me in Augsburg, Germany."

"Your? Say again. Did I hear what I heard?"

"A German girl, waiting for me in Augsburg."

"Seriously?"

"Yes, Captain, seriously."

"God*damn*. Weird enough, but fair enough. Let's go then."

4.

They were drunk or close to it, the sergeant and the captain, having reached the bottom of a gallon of local wine, a pulpy drink that could be chewed a little before swallowing. Their jeep was parked in a dry creek bed, near the decrepit Italian hamlet Bellsignana, out of sight in case they got too drunk, and since their partnership months before had been planned in the seclusion of a jeep, so it continued. The captain, betrayed by a relaxed state of loopiness, was slipping into forbidden questions he had never wanted answered before. "Hey there, tell me. Tell me how you ever picked up those German field maps."

"Not important," said the sergeant.

"But I want to hear about it for once."

"I bring back crap all the time."

"Crap? This wine is crap. German field maps are a *treasure*. Losing them is a *disaster*. You didn't find these things waiting by themselves under a tree somewhere."

"Under a tree."

"Under a tree. Hogwash. Look at me. Are you seeing straight? Shucks, I can't tell 'cause I'm not seeing straight either. But hogwash."

"Well, the maps were under a tree."

"How *dangerous* was this? How goddamn dangerous was that goddamn tree?"

"I can't say how dangerous."

"You can't?" The captain tipped back a final swig, the sergeant the same, their lips and tongues stained a crude purple, and the jug was empty. "You can't. Why not, you can't?"

"Seems like at sometime, somehow, at someplace, or other, I lost the feeling for whatever danger is. Just lost it."

The view far to the northwest was of a mountain known in Italian as Mount Felicity, where lately sorrow had reigned instead. Captain Delaney at this instant felt in his bones why the other men, when eating in the mess tent, sat apart from the sergeant after nodding respectful hellos, their distance an instinct for a safety zone. The soldiers did prize their Geronimo, whose reconnaissance miracles brought fame to his military family, and yet, few men can sit easy around a spectre who prowls after sundown like a hungry vampire, and who will end up with a silver bullet in his own heart. "The jug's finished, right?" said the captain. "The goddamn jug. Listen, you can hear me. If I use a *please*, will you tell what went on that night. With the goddamn maps?"

"My same old routine. Same whoop-de-do. Wait for night, smudge up my face, wiggle though woods, slide-slide-slide past both front positions, way beyond."

"Risky," said the captain. "Very very risky."

"Once you reach the rear zone, it's easier. Nobody expects trouble from behind. Nobody checks backward. At daylight I hole up in the brush, eat my rations, nap."

"Risky. Very."

"Check around any battlefield and you find mostly blank space with plenty of hiding nooks, some comfortable. At nightfall here I come again, in reverse, directly up their backs."

"Jesus. You *are* crazy. Stop. You're scaring me sober. No, no, I mean go on, finish it. Go-go-go ahead, finish."

"I wait until two o'clock in the morning about, until it's blackest and coldest, when the Germans want to stay asleep, the same as our men do. Sometimes I think a tired soldier would rather die than wake up. Sometimes he does die. If I locate the shape of a map case, or anything special, I crawl in to snag it, and by crawling I mean slow as, say, twenty meters in an hour. That's the trick, being slower than the shadows. If a voice speaks out, I might answer. That's the best emergency trick, the mother tongue, the mother tongue that coaxes the fussy baby to close its eyes. I've had many conversations with voices from the dark, half in German, the other half in English when I meet our own sentries. Of the two, green GI's worry me the most."

Captain Delaney rolled his head back, neck blocked against the seat top. "I'm trying to picture this. I'm concentrating, sort of. You go creeping in. You might chat a bit. You take the goddamn maps. *Auf Wiedersehen.*"

"It was black as sin. No moon."

"No moon. Easy as pie."

"A rainy night with no moon is absolutely tops. I could steal their underwear."

With a clatter the captain rolled the jug over the jeep's door cutout, onto the gravelly ground. He scolded himself, "I'm another American litterbug in Europe. Empty shell casings and empty wine jugs covering a continent. Sarge, don't make me send back home the wrong kind of letter. Our business together isn't so much fun for me, nowadays, you should know. Whenever you vanish for a day, or *three* days, I think, goodbye, that's it, finally."

"Their underwear while they still had the underwear on, if that part wasn't clear."

"You have a mother and a kid brother or someone waiting back in California. They write. I saw the letters."

"No living mother or father. But there's a mothering older sister, who dotes on me, her son, my brainy kid nephew, both in California, her husband, a decent guy fighting out in the Pacific, Silke Wolke in Germany, a captain and sergeant stuck in Italy without any wine in a jeep with a white star on the hood. That's my summary."

"Silke Wolke. Huh? Oh, she's the one. Goddamn that wine for letting me ask about those maps and goddamn you for telling. That's my summary."

* * * *

Seasons shifted, locations to hide a jeep changed. On this Sunday afternoon, with the jeep's fabric top and panels in place, its windshield raised, a rain by itself created sufficient privacy. As window droplets congealed they turned into abrupt downward trails on glass, their unpredictability a silent entertainment. Today's superb vintage *Chianti Riserva* had to be commandeered by Major Delaney, whose excuse for the theft was celebrating an advancement in rank and his reassignment to France as tactical liaison officer with a regimental HQ staff. The new major was considered a super-duper prospect, he told the sergeant, "the most successful young officer in this sinkhole Italian campaign." The major handed over authentic crystal stemware for the wine. "But we both know I owe my brilliance, and my career, to you."

"Don't puff it up."

"I'm not. Puffing it up I'm not, my good friend. What grates on me is how to give you credit without pitching both of us into hot water. Anyhow I'm guessing that you've got a reward suggestion for me. Whoosh, this ambrosia goes down quick, eh? Listen to this crystal ring." He pinged his empty goblet rim before refilling.

The sergeant, after his own refill, said, "And you guessed right about a reward. Take me along to France. Put me and keep me in a spearhead unit. Advise my company commander that I'm strictly recon and will report to Major Delaney through him. Congratulations, Major, by the way. A shiny gold oak leaf suits you. Lovely foliage."

The new major finished his glass. "Wait, what am I doing, gulping this expensive wine." He poured his glass full again. "I'm sipping now. Oops, not sipping."

"With these mountains in Italy," said the sergeant, "and the Alps up ahead, we won't make it into Germany before the war ends. In my opinion, the big push will roll across the flatlands of France and Belgium."

"With armor and air cover."

"Let's drink to a fast dash to German dirt."

"You and me."

"The sergeant and the major. Congratulations again."

"How do I pull off your transfer?"

"The smartest young officer in Italy has only a minor request. You West Pointers always chum together. The brotherhood of the best. Terrific wine."

Major Delaney was already refilling both glasses. "Goddamn terrific wine." Looking through a crack around the jeep's side curtain, he checked the soggy grass below, the mud in the field, inhaling its smell, imagining the sticky goo back at camp, and not forgetting that the sergeant had previously announced he was scouting tonight because of this weather. "Sarge, don't be offended. But I wonder if I can handle the responsibility of you anymore—to spell out my worries in capital letters. This week I discovered three or four white hairs, at my age, and I don't own that much hair anyway in the first place."

"Fill us up. Then drink up."

"Don't go out tonight, Sarge. Let's take a break. We can coast for a while."

"Drink up. I'm headed to France."

"Why do I do this, letting you go out again in the night? I can break a promise. Why don't I order you to stay?"

"Because you know why *I* do it, and besides, the major intends to be a light colonel before we reach the Rhine and a full bird colonel before we leave Europe altogether."

Major Delaney did drink up. "God*damn* it. You turned me into a drunk."

"Goddamn it."

"Goddamn me especially. If you let yourself be killed, I'll fry in hell, and deserve it. Stay alive. Stay alive at least until I make lieutenant colonel, which could ease my sins a little. What's this burbling in your Chianti. Am I such a joke?"

"Negative. I laugh when the major is good, when the wine is good, and when Geronimo gets an overnight slog in a rain poncho."

* * * *

While Major Delaney always had expected this day, he felt a blow, and an unprofessional pain, when their last private meeting happened, late 1944 with their American units in grimy snow on the pastured fields of Belgium, waiting for suitable weather and the assault into Germany. Instead of sitting in a jeep, the major and sergeant sat in the heated kitchen of a stone farmhouse. Instead of stealing a select wine to celebrate the major's approval for another promotion, they smoked expensive cigars and cozied up to the stove. "Passing out cigars," said Major Delaney, "is the honored custom for announcing new babies or new lieutenant colonels, I forget which."

"Make it then for a baby lieutenant colonel. I don't notice any other colonels your age around here."

Through their twin streamers of cigar smoke the major, observing across the table, already experienced a sinking of spirits. Possibly the bleak icy sky behind the windows on this cheerless Sunday had its effect, but the sergeant himself showed a bleakness. He fit the standard storybook illustration of a Wild West frontier hunter gone feral: too gaunt, too unwashed, quiet from too much solitude. The top half of an ear was missing. A grizzly could have chewed it off in a tussle, although another sort of beast did the job, a Mauser MG42, recognizable by its deep coughing growl at 1200 bites a minute. "Goddamn it," Major Delaney had bellowed out from afar when he saw the bandage and spoke softer, much later, when touching the curled scar tissue. "Close, close, close. Like I said before, you deserve another medal, but goddamn it, why the Purple Heart?"

They snacked on fresh baguettes and potent cheese, an acquisition equal to the cigars. "You never fail to be an A-1 provider of treats," said the sergeant. "And of favors. New boots, new transfers. And now your last favor for me. Please."

The major lurched, mistakenly set his cigar down on the wrong plate, dusting the baguettes with ashes. "Sure. I think."

"I need to be put into the best possible combat position for Augsburg, Germany."

"So soon. Has that time really come already? Lord, can I even find Augsburg on a map?"

"Here's my best condensed schoolhouse lecture. Ready for it? Augsburg is located near Munich at the confluence of the Wertach and Lech rivers, founded 15 B.C. by Roman emperor Augustus, population now 185,000, Mozart's father born there, Silke born there. Today she still lives there, along with its fabric mills, acetylene producers, machine factories, and unfortunately the Messerschmitt aircraft works. The Huns destroyed Augsburg in the 5th century, Charlemagne in the 8th, the kingdom of Bavaria in the 11th, now American and Brit bombs in the 20th. Reassign me to the end of our southern flank, the 3rd or 7th Army, or whoever will lead into Bavaria. Check with the big brass and pull all your strings for me, will you?"

"Goddamn. Is my head nodding? I feel my head nodding YES, even though you're a habit I'd prefer not to break. And you just spoiled my celebration party, incidentally."

"No, no," said the sergeant. "For that I'm sorry."

"Hey, old friend. I look at you and don't like what I'm seeing. I see a beat-up soldier who's lost maybe twenty pounds, has dirt under his fingernails, and in general looks like a pile of barnyard fertilizer."

"This dirt and I are very good buddies. We travel everywhere together, have for months."

"I intend to ask you to do *me* a last favor. Allow me to arrange a two-week furlough in Paris, or London . . . better London, if I can manage London. Spend two weeks soaking your fingernails and the whole rest of you in a hot soapy bathtub. Don't wag your head NO."

"Am I wagging my head?"

"You wag your head without wagging your head. Two short weeks. A favor to me?"

"Anything else and I would. Anything else. But thanks. And thanks for the booze you bought and stole and shared. Thanks for letting me roam far and wide. Thanks for not asking questions. Thanks most for all those worried *goddamns*—they were goddamn authentic, I know."

"Here's my hand. Let's shake. I want you to find what you want to find, if that makes sense. Where's that booze when we need some?"

The soon-to-be colonel and the sergeant leaned across the table for their handshake, avoiding the dishonesty of saying, "We'll get soused together again after the war."

5.

Today in Germany is, and feels, like springtime, with a cheery April sun and warmth by mid-morning, more green on the ground than mud for once, birds everywhere on the wing. Germany wants the hard winter to stay away and never come again. Four American soldiers move through the sylvan landscape on an advance probe into unknown territory, across wooded slopes above Swabian valleys, in the direction of Munich. In the lead is the sergeant. Behind him come the other three, each age twenty, one from Texas, one from Utah, one from New Hampshire, each on tiptoes like trespassing hikers. Nobody intends to die and ruin such a lovely postcard day when the war is already good as won.

Whenever a farm building or house appears, the reconnaissance team edges to higher terrain and scans below with binoculars. Other than an abandoned *Kugelwagen* jeep the *Wehrmacht* has left no trace, and the fighting apparently will resume farther ahead, at Ulm or Augsburg and the buffer strip around Munich. Now the American scouts are scheduled to turn back, and the soldier from Utah calls softly, "Whatcha think, Sarge?" The one from Texas adds, "Past 11 hunnert hours, Sarge." And the sergeant halts until they bunch together, the private from New Hampshire unpeeling a chocolate bar, everyone waiting for instructions.

The sergeant reviews their return route because he will stay behind as usual. He says, "Tell the captain not to wait for me, and I'll turn up when I turn up, and if I don't turn up, put me down as MIA. Tell him under no condition to stop and search for me. Who knows, maybe I'll meet you boys later in Berlin for the victory party." The soldiers have anticipated this sort of briefing, given the extra fullness of the sergeant's pack, just as they expect their captain once again to cuss before tossing up his hands in resignation. The boy from Texas, an unspoken admirer, would join the sergeant, almost, but lacks the nerve to go along, let alone the nerve to ask. None of them wishes the sergeant good luck. General Medals Corporation, drinker of German blood since North Africa, needs no luck: sneak a peek at those metallic eyes, at his skin weathered into a piece of animal hide, at that ear torn away—bitten off by an SS sniper he had choked to death the scuttlebutt was.

Instead of a goodbye the men share their food snacks with the sergeant. In the middle of this social pause he disappears, blending into forest patterns with his camouflaged paratrooper pants, olive wool cap snug over his hair. On their return trip, Utah, Texas, and New Hampshire hurry along, nagged by a confidence slump without Geronimo from San Francisco in the lead.

* * * *

By himself the sergeant moves faster, winding through screens of Black Forest pines and firs, orienting his memorized map toward 122 Adlersweg. Late in the afternoon at a musical mountain rill split by a thrust of boulders, and sent splashing down into separate ravines, he hides himself, uses his pack as a pillow, and falls asleep listening to the free lullaby. With darkness he is on his feet again. Despite all the splendid stars, under the forest canopy the night has contracted into syrupy black, allowing him safe passage on a wide hillside path abandoned by anything human, or at least by sensible people afraid to be caught at dark where the brothers Grimm found witches and wolves on the loose. The sergeant lets a few of their folktales occupy his mind, and the miles pass by.

At dawn, into the daylight, he remains on the open path, parallel to a road in the valley below. This exposure could be risky, but Germany seems deserted. The sergeant calculates that two more days at this rapid pace will find him closer to Augsburg than to his own American troops, and that city, broken apart, was ripe for his invasion, with or without the U.S. Army. Throughout the day he does not stop or leave the path until his afternoon rest. During the next long night he hurries over the foot trail, taking out a poncho when a chill shower hits, and he walks faster yet, in defiance of the wet, eating on the go. The rising sun at dawn scatters the nighttime clouds into salmon-and-soot colors, finally with the passing hours chasing them altogether away, leaving behind the bluest sky and warmest day of the season.

At noon the sergeant notices in the distance a collection of roofs—a village surrounded by plots of farm fields—and shifting into the forest cover as he approaches, he uses this opportunity to sit, concealed, and finish a meal of K-rations. He tries to count the number of cows being herded by a farmer through a gate. The total is either eight or nine. Finding a dry cloth in the pack he wipes down his M2 and cleans the ammo clip, inserting it back into the rifle. The smell of fresh metal, as part of a customary routine, reminds him to brush his teeth, rinsing his mouth afterward from the hip canteen filled with brook water. Deciding to count those cows exactly he hauls out the binoculars. Eight cows. There are eight cows, and tucked behind the barn's corner, under a ramshackle lean-to, is a *Schützenpanzerwagen* 251 armored half-track, painted German field gray, complete with a 20mm *Flak* mounted on its anti-aircraft pedestal. Removing his pack the sergeant angles in a serpentine drift down toward the village. Binoculars out again he locates several more *SdKfz* 251's squirreled away in ambush positions, these equipped with 37mm *Pak* cannons. Over there, under camouflage netting beside a rustic cottage where somebody's grandmother was presently hanging out her laundry to dry, stands a short row of 75mm light artillery pieces. All the gear, all the visible soldiers in their matched uniforms, display a legitimate fighting *Wehrmacht* unit, not a nest of stragglers, and the sergeant decides they have orders to delay his own advance column of Americans—metaphorically, a frantic strike by a cornered snake just as a boot stomps down to crush its head.

Uphill at his pack again, he sits, gathering up his equipment and his thoughts before he pulls out of here for Augsburg. The sergeant has no desire to reverse his direction and make the trek back for a military report. Let the U.S. Army end the war without him. Let him clear his mind of this war—he never liked it anyway—and leave room inside only for images of 122 Adlersweg and a happy August filled with days also bright and warm, as this April day is.

So potent are his activated visions of 1941 they invent a deception. Because the sergeant hears Silke's voice speaking aloud, her actual voice, or a female German voice that could have been heard at a picnic on the grassy banks of the Lech River. And it is a real voice. He aims himself at the sound, leaving behind the pack to burrow quietly through the tightest thickets, ending at the edge of a small open circle near the pathway. Brush arching overhead, the sergeant lies there flat on his stomach in the spongy rot of last year's leaves, his chin resting on the sideways M2.

Out in the cleared space, on a blanket, a young couple in an appropriate coincidence is finishing a picnic, marmalade and rolls, a modest imitation of the Wolke family feast. The girl wears a traditional dirndl frock that seems out of place in a forest, with flared sleeves and full skirt, pale in color, decorated by pink embroidery down the bodice. Her companion has on a baggy militia uniform, the pants held up by a civilian belt, and street shoes instead of regulation boots. Speaking in an ardent mush of Swabian diphthongs the boy is praising the girl's hair. "Gretel" he calls her, proving that the Grimm brothers knew their business hereabouts. Her hair does deserve approval, with a rich maple sheen from the wavering sunbeams, its single heavy braid, meticulously woven and laid forward over a shoulder, falling under its own weight to lodge into the focus line between her breasts. The embroidery there at the bodice depicts pink flowers on green vines. She approximates the age of Silke Wolke back when Silke first walked into the lecture hall at Stanford, but unlike that sylph from Augsburg, this girl's image suits her dirndl dress. Her face has a healthy, buttermilk-fed, country maiden's complexion, her lips and the entire fulsome body voluptuous at this early stage before it soon passes into comfortable plumpness. The boy wishes to kiss those lips, he says. She permits it without showing excitement. "I think about you always," the boy tells her, "and that makes me feel very good." He places an awkward arm around her shoulders. Somberly, she lectures him, "Whenever the shooting starts, duck down and stay down, if you can. Dieter, keeping out of it is the best idea."

They continue talking, with interference from an occasional kiss, the girl channeling the topic into further cautionary advice. To concentrate the sergeant closes his eyes, following the complex musical score of her German cadences. He knows it has been a lifetime since he last pressed his fingertips against Silke's throat, registering there her words and her heartbeat, a mixture he could never forget, but which feels in April 1945 more and more like only touching a dream about a dream. Her last words to him had been written, not spoken. In 1942 came a letter from Augsburg to California, via Lisbon, Portugal, when such a contact was still possible, and the letter rushed him that same day to an Army recruiting office. Silke's precisely chiseled handwriting, a calligraphy nearly, he had recognized with hurtful delight. The intent of her letter he had not recognized. "The big world has left our tiny world behind," she wrote, a storm of ambiguity hanging over that sentence, and this from a mind that by choice always insisted on clarity. She did not include the important word "love" above her signature. Unavoidable, how much the letter had frightened him, threatened him, with its demand for answers. Here was Silke Wolke seeking to protect him in some sacrificial way. Or here was Silke Wolke the pragmatic banker's daughter dealing out cold final facts.

* * * *

"*Grüß Gott, grüß euch*," intrudes a series of hellos from out front in the clearing, as a German patrol enters in its tactical file, 1, 2, 3, 4, 5, 6, 7, 8 soldiers appearing, one for each of the farmer's cows. All are armed with front-line weapons, the *Gewehr* 43, an *Obergefreiter* even carrying a *Sturmgewehr* MP 44, the best attack rifle in the world and a gun the sergeant would be using himself had he collected enough German ammunition. These soldiers, hardly older than the boy, appear a generation beyond, from the grime deepening their facial creases, from that fatigue, that surrendered fatalism in their body stance. The sergeant is familiar with these dangerous hallmarks and he carefully rotates his M2, safety off, from under his chin toward the crowded meadow.

The group chats about the nice weather, makes introductions, the soldiers identifying their unit, as does the boy, who offers how he got lucky with a two-day home pass for his mother's birthday. A soldier extends a pack of cigarettes, clipped into halves. "Thanks, no," says the boy. Another soldier unwraps a square of marzipan for the girl, which the boy also declines on her behalf. The soldier insists, "I want her to have it. Here, my last piece of sweets." "No—" begins the boy, but the girl, wiser, steps up and takes a bite, performing a conciliatory "Mmmm . . ." She switches her braid from the breasts to down her back, prompting a soldier to announce, "Such a pretty girl," more a rash observation than compliment. The boy declares, "She's my fiancée."

A significant quiet settles over the clearing, suspending movement, and talk, until a soldier breaks in with his troubled calendar calculations. "The last German girl I kissed was . . . a year ago, April, 1944." Another soldier recalls summer 1943 as his last kiss in Germany, and since then only Polish or French whores. "Wait now," complains the boy, "no foul language, for the sake of my fiancée" and the girl tells him, "Dieter, never mind about that." The soldier in command, a *Feldwebel*, a rank identical to the sergeant's, comments without malice, "Your fiancée, my ass. Your two-day pass, my ass. Nobody gets passes anymore. Germany has a rope around its neck and we're all choking, or didn't your mother explain that at her birthday party?"

"My dear young lady," suggests the soldier with the marzipan chunk, "all my candy, every crumb of it, for a kiss on your palm. I ask as a gentleman."

The boy eyes the exit routes, reciting aloud the hours and minutes the girl is already overdue at home, when someone instructs him, again calmly, to stop lying. "We know what you're after here in the weeds with her, Dieter. We're men, too." A new soldier proposes, probably as a joke, "All the candy, all our cigarettes, all our cash—worthless these days but take it—and what we ask is for some German soldiers to smell a German girl's hair." The boy demands, "I won't permit more talk like this. Won't."

"Dieter*chen*, close your trap," says the *Feldwebel*, his voice at a level now below even calmness, down to indifference, and he bows to the girl with weary reasonableness. "You're a patriot, aren't you? Of course. Shouldn't a countrywoman permit her brave countrymen to smell her clean hair? So little would mean so much. The day after tomorrow the Americans arrive, or the next day, or the next at the latest—"

The boy shouts. His vocal pitch cracks like the youth he is, losing its male timbre. "You pigs! You'll be reported for these threats!"

Instinctively the soldiers react to this abrupt noise, checking around in their survival habit, over their shoulders, into the woods, at the sergeant. But shortly they are chuckling when the boy repeats, "I'll report you myself!" The soldiers say, "Will you tattle to Field Marshal Kesselring or go direct to Berlin and Mr. Hitler? Please tell him how you went AWOL to bang this girl."

Holding her fingers out the girl hushes her friend, and he makes use of this gesture by gripping her hand, leading the two of them away. A quick expert stab with a rifle butt breaks the boy's nose, sinking him to his knees. "Ouch, too bad for the kid," says a soldier, apparently meaning it, with another soldier wondering, "Christ, is this all leading somewhere?"

The girl aids the boy to a seat against a tree. Blood gushes desperately, those pink flowers on the girl's bodice lost in spreading stains of red, and she staunches the bleeding with her skirt hem. Meanwhile violence has awakened the soldiers from their lethargy and the sight of the girl's soiled dress plainly disturbs them. "The thing is ruined. What a helluva day. We should soak the dress to save it, yes? Steinhauer, your family runs a laundry."

When the soldier, apologizing, makes to examine the bloody fabric the girl shrinks aside, and up struggles the boy, flailing about like a circus clown with a ruptured tomato for a head. A mere shove flattens him again. Most sorry, say the soldiers to the girl, please forgive us, forgive such a terrible embarrassment to you, but the dress must come off. She undoes the hooks, fingers trembling, the halting progress of her slow fumbles, perversely, an allure. Pulling the dress up and over, the girl presents it to the two soldiers who have their canteens ready, and she stands in a muslin chemise, also bloodied, refusing to remove it. But a soldier respectfully inches off the undergarment. The clothing is twice saturated and wrung out, and draped with fussy precision over a limb to dry by the former laundryman. What remains in her nakedness is the blood on her hands, arms, chest, shins, feet, which she washes by herself from a canteen. "Okay, okay," declares someone, "we're finished."

No, there are soldiers with something left to solve. They behave in the manner of certain visitors in an art museum, those novices who squint, perplexed, at a sculpture they might understand if they should step closer or change the angle of their heads or think harder. One of them asks the girl to unfasten her braid. She hesitates, before scooping the braid forward to unlock each knot, letting the hair fan out in rippled kinks as a partial cover for her breasts. This common bedroom action amounts to a revelation. Now the soldiers remember who this statue is and now the girl has eight different names besides Gretel.

"Dortmeier," calls out the *Feldwebel*. "Dorti, you can be the first to touch the girl's hair." The soldier instead politely requests, please *Herr Feldwebel*, if he might be excused to return early to camp. Permission is granted. After the departure, the *Feldwebel* feels obligated to inform the girl, "In February, Dortmeier's wife was firebombed in Dresden. On Valentine's Day, funny enough."

The soldier who last kissed a German girl in 1943 volunteers to kiss a German girl again. Another soldier says, "Hold on. What are we then, a gang of Ivans out raping helpless German women? Wake up. The *Wehrmacht* punishment for raping even a Polish woman is execution by firing squad. And I had to line up and watch that happen in 1940." The first soldier answers, "Who claims a kiss is raping," and another soldier, the *Obergefreiter* with the *Sturmgewehr*, slaps its stock. "Stop at kissing, will we? What an afternoon. I don't want any piece of this, none." He walks away, crouches down, hunched against his thighs. Another soldier says, "The point is, in a couple of weeks the Yanks and the Reds are going to take what we're only yakking about. The Reds will just hop on her and the Yanks will buy her with a pair of nylons and a big toothy grin." Another soldier says, "Naw, you blockheads. Think why our unit got dumped behind. Think about eating six feet of dirt. That's the real point. Tell me, what'll we put in our empty fuel tanks to escape, our piss?" Another says, "Fuel or not, with these clear skies, the Mustangs will be strafing the meat off our bones."

A silent soldier is picked by the *Feldwebel*, "Because you, Joachim, are always patient and obedient, and because your home is in Königsberg, where your German family has been chased out and will never live again."

The soldier accepts his selection, its command imperative, and lays down his rifle, stepping in front of the girl, saying, "Look how clean she is. I got road crud on me." For all to notice, he is quaking as much as the girl, and under his tree the boy shakes the most. "I'll get her dirty, won't I?" An irritated voice speaks up, "Kiss her, Joachim, you moron. Grab her or something. We can't wait forever until our turn, you know."

The *Obergefreiter* hits the ammunition magazine of his MP44 with a slam of his hand. "Joachim, I'm prepared to shoot you."

"Point your weapon away, Corporal," orders the *Feldwebel*.

The *Sturmgewehr* stays on target. "I believe, yes, I'll plug any sonofabitch who touches her tits."

"Turn that weapon away," demands the *Feldwebel*.

"Joachim," says the *Obergefreiter*, "I like you a lot, but I'll put a round right into your scrawny rump and report it as a weapon malfunction. Joachim, I'm clicking off the safety."

"Horseshit," says the *Feldwebel* and instructs the soldier, "Go on with it," and the soldier takes a pinch of the girl's hair, samples its softness, and kisses that tiny bunch caught between his fingers. The pinch becomes a handful, the handful easily becomes two fistfuls, the kissing becomes tasting the hair as much as kissing, and the soldier's lips follow the flow of her hair down to the shoulders, down to her nipples.

The girl wails, "No shooting! No more blood! Nobody shoot!"

* * * *

This miniature German tragedy in the clearing could not turn any more dramatic, but it does. Out of nowhere and into the open appears the sergeant, his M2 unlocked and level at his hip, an explosive voice at top strength, deliberately putting back the American accent he had labored for years to erase: "*Halt! Keine Bewegung. KEINE! Passt ganz gut auf, meine Jungs,* here's an American soldier who'll gut-shoot you all unless those weapons drop to the ground—slowly, slowly, *schön langsam, schön langsam!*"

Slow they have to be, because the seven of them, the nine, are a tableau of utter shock. What in God's world was *this*, standing there, threatening in German, muck and leaves stuck to his front, outfitted like a forest bandit instead of a soldier, or like a raggedy scarecrow that walked itself up here from a farmer's field down below. But the scarecrow holds a real American rife, a deadly real Winchester automatic buzz gun, and the scarecrow does really scare. The German soldiers let their weapons fall, except for the *Obergefreiter*, swinging around his *Sturmgewehr*, and the sergeant squeezes off a burst that kills him.

The Winchester's sharp chatter rings forth with an unmistakable alarm bell, bouncing copies of itself from mountainside against opposite mountainside, across the distance. Down in the valley bottom everything, and everyone, now knows there is trouble up in those woods, and raise their heads to search: the cows, the grandmother, the *Wehrmacht*.

Using the barrel of his M2 the sergeant directs the soldiers into a cluster, ordering them to strip down and "get as bare as the girl." When the scowling *Feldwebel* hesitates, up snaps the Winchester and the uniforms with underwear fly off in a flurry. "Now, friends," says the sergeant, "you have a choice. Either I shoot you anyway, or you can go, take the boy with you, and promise to have your medic fix his nose. Can you repeat *promise*? Louder. Good, my friends, good. Your clothes stay here. The girl stays here."

Left behind together in their little meadow the sergeant and the girl exchange a stare of mutual puzzlement and suspicion. With the return of stillness to the sunny afternoon the birds, knowing no better, start to sing again.

"Don't be afraid," he tries to reassure the girl, "I won't repeat what they were doing to you." The sergeant retrieves the girl's undergarment and dress, advising, "clammy still," and she accepts assistance fitting into the clingy corners. "Well, Gretel," he says, "an ugly day in an ugly war. May I sit by you?" Her wordless astonishment he takes as consent. "Since I overheard your name already, I'll introduce myself. Sergeant Geronimo. Too bad I'm not Hansel, that would make a fine pair of us, wouldn't it?" He tells her she is free to leave although he wishes her to stay, for a few minutes at least. First, the sergeant explains, he must examine the soldier he just killed. "Gretel, the *Obergefreiter* was the one I most hoped wouldn't make a move at me, but the one I thought who most would."

The *Obergefreiter* is a broken slumped pile of knees and elbows, and the sergeant rolls the pile over, face up, because this skinny kid resembles Stefan Wolke. It is not. At the chest a sodden circle of crimson indicates where a skilled Sergeant Geronimo, under extreme pressure, had placed a tight pattern of four bullets. The sergeant debates why he killed this youngster, why he did not keep himself hidden and safe in the brush, as he had two hundred times before. Was it to protect the girl, or hurt her, yes hurt her, with a bloody sight after she had shrieked out "No more blood!" Both questions made sense to him. Any answer made equal sense.

The girl is likely even more surprised than the sergeant that she sits there, waiting for him. He thanks her for the surprise. He joins her, alongside, and shows no interest whatsoever in hurrying away from danger. "Believe it or not, Gretel, I once *memorized* more German poetry than you probably *read* in school." The sergeant recites several stanzas of Schiller, from some of Silke's favorite lines. "In France I lifted a copy of Schiller from a dead German lieutenant, who wore eyeglasses with one lens missing. I attempted to tack together a political symbolism about that lieutenant and his glasses . . . without any success."

The girl half listens to this opaque rambling while her wide eyes stray over to the tree trunks, where she may have seen shifting shapes already.

"Gretel, about my namesake, did your author Karl May ever put Geronimo in any of those ersatz American westerns of his about the Indians? Geronimo was a kind of nuisance guy, also an Apache. For punishment, the Mexican soldiers executed Geronimo's mother, wife, and young children, and for revenge he struck back, and for revenge the Mexicans struck back, and for revenge, *et cetera.* So am I the Apache or the Mexicans? Take a guess."

The girl points to the trees. "They'll shoot you."

"And I've been shot before." The sergeant tugs his partial ear. "This poor boy, Dieter. He's not your fiancé although he wants to be. No offense to him but you can do better is my judgment, after spending an hour viewing you. A spunky fellow anyhow. The strangest thing is, Gretel, I have a fiancée practically a stone's throw from here, in Augsburg. *Augsburg,* how's that for a joke. We never had an engagement ring or any of the usual rigmarole. We just had what we had."

"I'm afraid," says the girl. "Please run, sir."

The birds, in their eternal innocence, continue singing. The sergeant looks at her closely. "You're young, I suppose, but getting older by the minute. Gretel, you'll fit your country perfectly after this war."

"Please," says the girl, "please run. I can't stop them, never."

He agrees. "When they see that body behind me they won't stop. How can we blame them in the end."

"Please," she says.

"I'm sorry."

"Please don't make me watch, sir."

"I apologize. I do."

"Don't make me see it."

"You can go, Gretel."

"I'll shout at them."

"You'll shout. You'll cry. You're almost crying now."

"*Please*, sir."

"Forgive me. This is cruel. Forgive me that you have to be the one. *Tut mir schrecklich leid.* But I need a German girl's tears right now, immediately, no more waiting."

The birds stop singing and Gretel obliges Spencer Lemay.